I0626627

THE HANDS THAT PULL THE STRINGS

Also by JS Carter Gilson

Fiends of the Hub

The Loneliness of the Deep Space Cargoist
The Languid Belly of the Beast

JS CARTER GILSON
THE HANDS
THAT PULL
THE STRINGS

Cavia *Porcellus*

NASHUA, NH

Cavia Porcellus
Nashua, NH

Copyright © 2021 JS Carter Gilson
All rights reserved.
Printed in the USA on demand.

ISBN 978-1-95504-502-5

Design by Cavia Porcellus.
Cover features illustrations furnished by Deposit Photos,
http://www.depositphotos.com/

For Otis and Cali
and siblings everywhere.

But something better happen soon
or it's gonna be too late to bring you back.

—*R.E.M.,* (Don't Go Back to) Rockville

1

Twin suns beat down through a cloudless, but hazy, sky. Inez was exhausted just walking to the shore. She was definitely more accustomed to the controlled atmosphere of ships and stations, and even of most planets. Sweat was dripping off of her brow and down her back and it was uncomfortable.

Coming here had been a mistake, she knew that now. There had to be another way to get what she was looking for, a way that didn't involve 43 degree heat and 100% humidity. At least the oxygen in the atmosphere was slightly higher than she was used to, and the gravity was .9 of standard. She thought that was good. She was having trouble remembering anything through discomfort.

She'd been on this moon for six days, and there was nothing she had liked about it. This was the last time she was going to that travel agent. This was supposedly a luxury resort, but there were almost no walls, no air conditioning, a hot ocean, nightly thunderstorms, and people. So. Many.

People.

Alright, the all-inclusive booze and food wasn't so bad, but here she was, on the black sand beach, the two stars of Procyon overhead, completely naked (due to local custom, any sort of covering was forbidden on the beach) and miserable. She didn't even have Lui on the moon with her, due to the mechanotron having issues on sand. She had a Sta-Cool canteen, a beach towel with the resort's logo on it, a folding beach chair and a can of spray-on UV blocker.

The beach was packed with people. Mostly it was humans, but there were a few non-human people around. A ruby-red Kastakallan stood out the most. They (Inez had trouble with Kastakallan genders, mostly because she didn't run into them very often) were well over two (two-and-a-half?) meters tall with three arms and two legs, which she thought meant it was a mercilan, the bearer of young, but she also thought that mercilans were rarely seen outside the household, so who knew, really?

Kastakallans were a bit hard to get used to looking at. Their torsos were sort of a prism, with a shoulder in front, and two a little behind their heads. Their heads could also turn 290 degrees, so you didn't always know which side you were facing.

This one was standing next to a human so pale she was practically translucent. Her hair was shaved on one side, and long on the other, dyed a green so unnatural it glowed in the light of multiple suns. She was slim, maybe a few years younger than Inez, and cute as fuck. She found herself making her way over toward them before she made a conscious choice.

She saw a third member of their party as she got

closer, a teen-aged human boy (maybe eighteen?) who was only slightly taller than the woman (who was closer to Inez's height), but had darker coloring. He was trying to grow a beard, but it wasn't exactly impressive. His hair was cropped close.

Inez saw a patch of bare sand right next to this group, so she spread out her towel and pressed the release button on the chair. It sprang open, and it took every amount of cool that she possessed to not jump. Her new neighbors didn't seem to have noticed.

The chair, which went from a flat 20 cm square to a comfortable, if low-slung, seat with a parasol, weighed almost nothing. Inez sat, and was immediately less concerned about people looking at her. For one thing, being lower to the ground all on its own meant she felt less exposed. Also, there was a natural ridge just a meter away from her giving some privacy. Now you could probably just barely see her hair from the other side.

"Excuse me," she heard next to her ear (the right ear, which was still a bit sensitive after getting repaired a week before). She again managed not to jump out of her skin. It was the Kastakallan, and now that Inez was closer, she was sure it was a mercilan. What was the right pronoun? Fuck.

"Hi," she said, after a moment.

"My friends and I are at an impasse."

Inez now saw at all three of them clearly for the first time. She could tell that the one she'd taken for a boy was actually nearer to the woman's age, but the wispy beard made a bit more sense when she saw him up close. Humans getting born into a gender that wasn't right was not a new thing, but it was often handled at a much younger age. Given what she knew (which was, admittedly, not much), she thought that he must have emerged within the last couple of years. He might not have even started gene therapy.

Also up close, despite their difference in skin tone, she could see a definite resemblance between the two humans.

Inez's attention went back to the Kastakallan. "Sorry, what's that?"

Mei smiled (that was it, mei/mer/them), and the young man rolled his eyes. The woman smacked him on the arm.

"Artur," mei indicated the young man, "wants to swim. Caiti," mei pointed to the equally young woman, "just wants to lie in the sun."

"And what do you want?"

"My needs are unimportant."

"Right," she said slowly. "Okay, and why can't they just do whatever they want? It's a free moon. Mostly."

"I am their guardian, and neither is allowed to be more than 100 meters away from me at any time."

"Guardian? How well does that pay?"

"I am indentured to their family until my crimes are paid off."

"I'm Inez. What's your name?"

"My name is unimportant."

The woman, Caiti, spoke up at this point. "We call mer Guardian. Mei won't tell us mer name either."

"Well, it's nice to meet you all. I myself have no interest in going into the water. I've heard there's fish here that are bigger than Guardian, and I'm not interested in being something's supper."

Caiti smiled triumphantly at her brother. "Fine," he grumbled, and sprayed himself down with UV-blocker.

"Why do you two need a guardian?" she asked Caiti, who moved her chair closer to Inez. She was so pale, Inez could see blue veins through her skin.

"Our parents insist on treating us like children," she said. "Our mom is the president and CEO of Magellanic Holos."

"Your mom is Beatriz Oliveira?"

"The one and only. Thank god. We do not need more than one of her. Mom and the dads send us away for a few months every year because she keeps making babies and doesn't want us hanging around. And there's always some guardian to keep us in line. Mei's cool, though." Guardian nodded mer head forward in acknowledgment.

All this time, Artur was flexing his muscles (which were nicely toned across his body, Inez noted) and stretching before laying down on the towel.

"I don't think I've ever seen her pregnant," she mused.

"Oh, no, you wouldn't. Whenever our dads knock her up, she uses an exowomb to gestate. She's got so many kids now, but most of them are off at boarding schools."

"Not to be indelicate, but why are you still living under her roof?"

"Better than the alternative?" offered Artur.

"What my, uh, brother means is, if we move out, we lose our allowances. We have to work."

Inez scowled. "I see. A fate worse than death."

"No, not like that," Artur said, picking up Inez's distaste. "We were taught virtually nothing. We have zero skills to offer anyone. We are a drain on society."

"So," Caiti picked up, "we do our civic duty and spend shit-loads of euan all over the place.

"Including dropping several hundred euan here."

Inez took a sip from her canteen. She liked them, but boy were they trying to change that quickly. The Kastakallan was basically a slave here, and was very wisely staying out of it for the most part.

She knew (mostly from being unable to avoid celebrity gossip at different stations' news feeds) that Bea Oliveira lived on Toscata, which had outlawed slavery, but with some pretty big loopholes. Households could purchase the prison sentences of individuals (other than those with life sentences or death sentences) to work for them. By law, they could not be freed until the sentence had passed.

Kastakallan breeding triads were rarely separated, even when imprisoned, so that left Inez with some uncomfortable assumptions. Namely, mer two partners were most likely dead, and since mei was imprisoned by the Free Earth (mei had a brand on mer shoulder like the one Inez used to have), they were probably killed "resisting arrest".

No wonder mei just wanted to be known as Guardian.

"I guess that makes me lucky. This is the longest vacation I've had in five years, and that last one was not at such an e--" she was about to say expensive, but decided against it, "--a nice place."

It had actually been at a much nicer place, on the palace grounds with Ihuoma, but then it ended with them breaking up, and now Inez wasn't going to think about that anymore.

"Nah," Caiti said, "this place is a dump. We thought

the beach would be nice, but it's too fucking hot."

"That's why I want to swim," Artur said into his arms. He was lying on his stomach resting his head.

"The water is over 35 degrees. No way."

This had the sound of an old argument. Probably one that went back to their childhood. Inez had seen bonded pairs of cats like this, who absolutely loved each other but were always batting each other about the ears.

"I assume that if one of you goes into the water and the other stays here, bad things happen?"

"Guardian will get hurt. They didn't say how, just that it would be bad. We're not assholes."

"Not about this, anyway."

"Alright, my brother is too much of a loser to ask this, so I will. Are you matched?"

Artur back-handed Caiti across the shin (it was all he could reach). Inez actually laughed out loud. "Oh, hell no. I am the worst thing ever to happen to so many people." It wasn't that many, but better to put the thought out of these innocents' heads. "You're both cute, I'll give you that. My romantic life is a shit-show of epic proportions."

A shadow came over them, blocking one of the suns briefly. Inez looked up and saw a large ship, much larger than the usual transport that would be arriving to bring new guests. It seemed to be headed toward the city that was near the resort. (There were actual residents here, not just resort employees, but resort guests were encouraged to remain on the grounds and not venture into the crime-infested boroughs up in the hills. None of the guests really listened to that advice.)

The city was called Garminburg and it had a

spaceport where guests first set foot on the moon. People like Inez, who had their own ships, left them in orbit controlled by the valet-bots near the arrival station, while the majority of guests were deposited directly by their transports at the city.

This ship was definitely not a transport. For one thing, it was olive green and had the Free Earth insignia painted on its side in white. For another, it had enormous guns.

"What the fuck is a battle cruiser doing here?" she heard from behind her, and saw some of the others on the beach starting to pay attention as well. The woman who'd spoken was in her 60s or so, and had a rank tattoo above her left breast. She was a General, or possibly retired, and she looked pissed.

Caiti had barely looked up, and Artur was still lying face down. Guardian, though. Guardian had stood. Kastakallans had far better eyesight than humans, owing to their eyes' much wider aperture and millions more rods and cones on their retinas. And right now, mei looked terrified by what she was seeing.

"What is it, Guardian?"

This, from Inez, got Artur to get up to his knees, and Caiti to shield her eyes looking up towards the ship. Mei was shuddering, and not able to look a way.

Inez placed a hand on mer central arm, and mei looked down at her. "They cannot be here for me," mei said, mostly for mer own benefit.

"Is there a reason they might be?"

The siblings looked between each other. This clearly wasn't something they had expected either.

"I may be paranoid," mei said.

"Good to know."

The moment of curiosity seemed to have passed for everyone on the beach other than the Oliveiras, Guardian, Inez, and the old General. Inez was pretty sure that Artur and Caiti would be just like the rest if Guardian wasn't being weird.

The General was tall, olive skinned, and very fit, with bright, white hair very closely cropped. After a few minutes, she noticed Inez staring at her.

"What?"

"You didn't seem too enthused about the new arrival."

"I'm here to relax. Battle cruiser, that's not relaxing. They don't just pull up on a resort moon for R&R."

Artur stepped forward. "Maybe they just needed to stock up on, I don't know, UV blocker?"

"Aren't you optimistic?"

Guardian was still acting nervous. Inez grabbed mer wrist gently. "They aren't going to send a whole battle cruiser after you, no matter what you did. They prefer efficiency when it comes to taking you into custody."

The tall mercilan nodded, mer black eyes watery, but with a bit of relief.

"Whatever it is, I'm sure none of us is directly involved," Inez said, while a small voice nagged at her about the data core on her rig right at this moment. She hadn't even come close to plugging it in since the whole thing at the waystation, so they couldn't know she even had it, or that Lui was building a processor that could decrypt it. People had been killed by the Free Earth because of it, and she wasn't going to let their deaths go unpunished, but that was not why a battle cruiser was trying to land in a spaceport where it would never fit.

After a few more minutes, the General, who Inez realized she didn't even know the woman's name, sat back down, and Inez and Guardian soon followed suit.

"Oh, fuck," Caiti said, and jumped up from her chair to the bag that was holding down their towels. "I forgot all about these." She handed Inez a set of high-end binocs, with a bit of a sheepish look. "I was going to use them for people watching."

Inez took them, carefully. They looked about as expensive as her rig, and she did not want to go into more debt by breaking them. "No judgment from my end," she said, and raised them to her eyes. "Holy shit," she said, realizing she could make out individual people at the space port. The binocs were auto-focusing and auto-stabilizing, and Inez desperately wanted to own a pair.

She was looking up and down a phalanx of marines, each armed with a standard infrasonic sidearm, but also each with a heavy IS cannon strapped to their backs. They were standing about ten meters from an open airlock and a gangplank, which was as close as the behemoth ship could get to landing. It's thrusters were probably doing a number on the landing pad. This group of about fifty marines was armed well enough to take out a small city on their own. "Oh, that's bad."

She heard the General get up, and handed the binocs over to her. The older woman whistled. "Fucking hell."

"What is it?" Caiti asked, standing up again. Artur and Guardian were also up on their feet.

"I forgot to check. What's the status of this moon?"

"Neutral but unaffiliated," the General said, still staring through the lenses.

"Could be they aim to change that. May I?" Inez held a hand out and the General gave her the binocs again. She took another look, and saw a man stepping down the gangplank to review the marines.

"Oh, you are fucking kidding me."

The man was Colonel Abram Hynes. She realized she also recognized some of the marines as well.

"Hi, Dad," she muttered coolly. "Fancy seeing you here."

"What's that?" Artur asked. He was the closest of them to her, so he was probably the only one who actually heard what she said.

"Oh, just someone I'm probably going to kill some day." She had only met the marine colonel about a month before, while trying her damnedest to survive the Free Earth's attack on the waystation she'd been at. It was following that whole thing that she found out about their shared genetics. (It wasn't a relationship, and she damn well wasn't going to call it that.) She'd spent most of her life thinking her bio-dad was Admiral Cotton Ringwald, her mother's owner (and then her owner, and then her murder victim) (not murder, self-defense) (not that the prosecutors would have seen it that way).

Turns out, some other asshole (Hynes) had also raped her mother, but convinced himself that they were in love. Since she already had practice killing her father, it was bound to happen again.

There as a loud boom that made the beach shake, and Inez looked into the sky for the source.

It didn't take her long to find it, but that didn't help her that much. She didn't quite know what she was looking at. The new arrival had clearly caused the sonic boom when it hit the atmosphere, but it didn't look like a Free Earth ship. The wrong color, for one thing. It was purple. There were too many curves, almost like a spiny nautilus, or a pine cone that's been opened to release its seeds. Its rear end was glowing and getting brighter. She saw a flash from the underside of the ship. It was firing. It had to be firing at the cruiser.

She turned and looked back to the cruiser, where the marines were scattering in all directions. Then the cruiser was engulfed in white light.

"Shit, get down. Now." She pulled Guardian and Artur to the ground as she dove for it. The shock wave would be there in seconds.

2

Shock wave, then sonic boom, and then a return to a breathable air pressure passed almost faster than she could account for. She could feel bruising along her back-side that was definitely caused by the crushing pressure of the exploding ship.

Inez cautiously raised her head. She was still holding onto Guardian and Artur, who appeared no worse for wear. To her right, Caiti had also managed to get down before the shock wave hit, and to the right, the General was pushing herself upward.

At least the sudden increase in heat had removed some of the humidity. Inez felt a slight breeze on the back of her head, and reached up to feel. The hair that she had so carefully regrown over the past week had been burnt almost to her scalp in the explosion.

"Mother fucker," she growled, feeling the rest of her hair, which seemed to have emerged unscathed. Then she looked up.

The beach was no longer overburdened with living things. Other than a few here and there, almost everyone had been taken unawares. Closer to the city, as much as there was a city anymore, there was just sand, looking a bit grayer than it had earlier in the day. Then the deep, wet, red took over.

Inez felt her gorge rise and forced herself to turn around. Behind them it was worse, with jumbled body parts and the dead making an angry blanket all around them.

Caiti didn't have Inez's self-control, and did vomit. Artur had been clinging to Inez, but he moved to his sister and held her hair back.

"Was that the Hands of the Gods?" he asked, which seemed to make Caiti gag again.

"General?" Inez asked, deferring to an elder, even if she was Free Earth military.

"I have never seen a ship like that before. The ships we've seen have been constructed. Mathematical. Precise. This," she said, before trailing off.

"This looked like a pine cone made of conch shells." Inez looked in the sky where the ship had been. It must have left while the Free Earth ship was blowing up. "Is everyone alright? Able to walk?" She didn't really wait for an answer. "We need to get off this beach, and we need to get some godsdamn clothes."

They picked their way across the expanse of the dead, helping a few survivors and picking up an entourage as they went. It took them about an hour to get where the beach house had been.

There were a few banks of lockers that hadn't been completely destroyed. Inez's wasn't one of them. Most likely, the comfortable jumpsuit and ear bug communicator to her rig were in amongst the rubble. If she could get through to Lui, she might have a chance, but without that communicator she would need to find a radio to call off-world.

The Oliveiras were still hanging around with her, and still exhibiting signs of shock. The General, who, like Inez, was not lucky enough to have an intact locker, was digging in the debris.

Guardian produced a key from somewhere (Inez wasn't sure where, and the options weren't something she wanted to think about) and slipped it into one of the lockers. It beeped as it opened. The kids (Inez couldn't help thinking of them as being much younger than her) pulled their clothes out. Caiti had a gray and green body suit, while Artur was in a slightly more practical shirt and pants. Both were extremely casual. Guardian then pulled a robe out and slipped it over two of mer shoulders.

"I don't suppose you have any more clothes in there," Inez said, more statement than question.

Guardian looked Inez up and down, walked two lockers over, and punched the door in. Mei pulled out a body suit similar to Caiti's and handed it over. "That should fit."

Inez took it and started putting it on. "Exactly how good are your eyes?" she asked the Kastakallan. That actually got a smile out of the generally stoic Guardian.

The General came back over to the four of them, having found a too-tight t-shirt (with a rip above the chest) and a pair of slacks. She handed Inez a pair of boots. "I thought these might be useful."

Inez grabbed them quickly, and then looked at the others a little sheepishly. Guardian didn't care, and the Oliveiras were putting on their own shoes.

"Thank you, Gen-- You know, I don't even know your name."

"Priyam Krishnamurthy."

"Do you think the Hands have some completely new style of ship that they're just debuting after decades of this war?"

"They are inscrutable, but not that inscrutable. On the other hand, no pun intended, there are no other major powers capable of making a warship like that."

"In this arm of the galaxy, anyway."

General Krishnamurthy gave Inez a look that clearly said, "Oh, you sweet summer child." Inez shrugged her shoulders and looked over to her wards.

No, not her wards. They weren't her responsibility, and she couldn't start to take responsibility for everyone and everything that happened in her vicinity.

Artur was hugging Caiti from behind as she quietly sobbed. There were a couple dozen other people, all in various stages of shock and grief. The fact that Inez wasn't in shock was probably a warning sign of something, but she wasn't going to think too deeply about that right now.

They were hopeless. The war was just background noise to a large number of Free Earthers, and other than Priyam and Inez it looked like none had seen anything like it up close. Inez avoided the hot zones, but she'd had plenty of experience with things going straight to shit. The General would only have gotten that rank through direct involvement in the war.

"I think we need to try to find someplace safe. I don't suppose you've got any sort of communicator? Scanner?" The older woman made a gesture like she was emptying out her non-existent pockets. "Right. Guardian? Anything in the locker?"

Mei pulled away from the siblings and focused on the bank of lockers in front of mer. Then mei did the same with the two others that were still standing, before pulling the same move mei had when getting Inez her clothes.

"How did the cops get the drop on you?" Inez wondered aloud, and then realized mei could hear her. "You don't have to say. I'm too curious for my own good." Her mind turned to the data core on her rig. Lui had been taking the week to build the decryption machine so they could finally know what all the fuss was about. She just as quickly put the thought away. Surviving first.

The item Guardian had found was a ball that was deceptively heavy. When Inez took it in her palm, a display appeared in front of her. This was no toy. It was a high-powered scanner, and was almost certainly illegal, given that it could read bank chips and encrypted documents (she found several in the rubble).

The controls were fairly simple, and she had it pan out to show what was once Garminburg and was no more. She made it superimpose an image of what the city had been, including the Free Earth ship at the port, and the rings of destruction became clearer. They were a good three kilometers outside of the city, but there was nothing to block or break the blast between the ship and the resort.

There was one building that looked reasonably the same as it had before the attack. When she zoomed in, it had clearly lost every piece of glass and she could see bodies inside, but it was standing and didn't look about to collapse.

Inez got up on a bench that was still able to hold

weight. "Folks," she said, and several people looked toward her in confusion. She didn't blame them, she did this without even thinking about it and now it seemed like a bad idea. Still, she was in it now. "There's a lot we don't know right now. We don't know who attacked the Free Earth ship. We don't know why that ship was even here. We sure as fuck don't know why they attacked. But we also don't know if they'll be coming back, and if they do, we'll need to be someplace much safer than out in the open in the ruins of this beach house."

A few more people had looked up. Priyam had a look of mild surprise on her face, while Artur was still trying to console his sister, but looking up at Inez anyway.

"Our best bet is going to be in the city. There are some structures still standing there, and we're going to need shelter. The walk will probably take a few hours, so if you can find canteens and working water, now's the time for it. I'm going to head out in ten minutes or so. If you want to come with me, be ready to go."

It wasn't much of a rallying speech, but it would have to do. Most of the people had managed to find some form of clothing in the time since leaving the beach, and some towels to get some of the blood and grime off of them. The scanner was giving its best advice for a route out of the resort. It wasn't exactly a great option, but it was better than no option in the end.

Inez, along with the Oliveiras, Guardian, and General Krishnamurthy, started the exodus by climbing up over a pile of rubble, in the general direction of the city. At the top, she could see more clearly just how bad it was.

Parts of the city were just a wall of smoke. The

scanner was showing them the way forward, and there were definitely going to be some hard parts. There weren't a lot of bodies here, but she knew they would be coming. Inez had seen more than her fair share of dead bodies in her life, and she wasn't eager to see more, but that's the way that seemed to lead to safety, so that was that.

Caiti seemed to be doing better with something to actually do, even if that was just walking and trying not to trip over anything. Artur was extremely protective, but he was also very focused on the walking.

Inez moved back into the lead, walking next to Priyam. "So it's either the Hands or it's not the Hands."

"Those are the two options," the older woman said, with only a trace of a sigh.

"I know you're sworn to secrecy and all that, but if you'd ever seen a Hand, would you be able to tell me?"

"No, but I also have never seen a Hand."

"Yeah, that's what everyone says."

"You seem to have taken command here," the General said, not disapprovingly.

"It was an instinct, and I regretted it immediately."

Priyam chuckled, then followed up with, "I don't buy that. Which regiment were you with?"

Inez stopped. "What?"

"You have the bearing of a military training."

"Not even a little bit," she said, starting to walk again. She sighed. "That logo on your chest? I did have on one, but on my shoulder."

Now it was the General's turn to stop. "You were a prisoner?"

"No, I was a fully owned slave. And frankly, if the

Admiral's bearing worked its way into me, I would prefer to go in literally any other direction."

Inez kept walking, leaving a widening gap between her and the veteran.

Guardian caught up with Inez at that point, making sure that mer wards were close enough behind that mei wouldn't be injured. "I couldn't help overhearing. Were you forced into bondage?"

"I was born into it. My mother was sold to pay debts."

"Does she know you're free?"

"I'm not sure on the whole afterlife thing, so," she shrugged here, "maybe? She was murdered when I was 11."

"Is it murder when one such as us is killed?"

The question was rhetorical, probably. Inez still answered. "Legally, of course not. It's just another red mark in the ledger."

They walked on in companionable silence. The tall Kastakallan moved quite gracefully across the rubble, with an inner peace that didn't match the little she'd learned about mer so far.

The scanner chirped, and indicted a change in route. They turned to the left, around a mound that looked like a blown up picture of an ant hill, and down a short incline into a less devastated part of the city. This wasn't the destination she had planned, but it seemed like a good spot for a regroup.

General Krishnamurthy seemed to be thinking the same thing, so Inez allowed her to catch up. About twenty others had come along, with the rest electing to stay behind. When they were all together, Inez climbed up a bit of wall that was relatively solid.

"We've been walking for about an hour, if you can believe it. Time flies when you're scared shitless, right?" This didn't get much of a reaction. "We can rest here for a bit. It should be relatively safe from," she faltered here, then gestured around generally. "We've probably got about another hour or so before we really get into town. We're all in relatively good shape, I think mainly because if you were going to get injured in that blast, it was going to be fatal."

"Inez," the General intoned, *sotto voce*. Right, not bringing up the deaths of everyone they knew and loved.

"It'll be about fifteen minutes before we get going again, so sit and get comfortable, if you can."

She got down off the wall and sat with her back to it. Caiti and Artur sat down on either side of her. Caiti put her head on Inez's shoulder and closed her eyes. Artur was picking up small pieces of debris and chucking them at the wall opposite. Guardian and Priyam were still standing, chatting below her hearing.

Inez's heart rate was starting to get back into the healthier range for not moving. She put her arm around Caiti's shoulder and squeezed gently. When had she become a comfort to others? Why was she taking charge? Other than getting away and back to the rig, she didn't even have a stake in any of these people.

Except, they were people. They needed someone. And she was there. Was that all there was to it?

The scanner beeped at her. "Alright, folks. Time to get moving again."

Caiti startled when Inez moved. Inez noticed a little drool on her lips. "Come on, sleepyhead."

"Fuck. I was hoping this was the dream part."

"We're not good enough for the Gods to do that for us."

"Speak for yourself," Artur said from her other side. "I'm a fucking saint."

He held out a hand to his sister, and then one to Inez, to help them stand. One sun was working its way down towards the horizon, but the other was still quite high and hot. Everyone was covered in dust and sweat and ash and blood and fuck knew what else. They looked like they were in a war zone. Inez realized a second later that they basically were in a war zone, so it was apt.

She pulled out the scanner, which had adjusted their route again. She started them out climbing back up the incline and going left, to what she recognized as the main avenue through the city. The city had a couple of skyscrapers before the blast, such as they could be called that at 99 stories. Most of the rest of the buildings were older, smaller, and made of less-sturdy stuff, and they pretty much didn't exist anymore.

The humidity that had largely been obliterated by the explosion was creeping back in. Caiti was clinging to Inez's arm as they walked, which slowed her down a bit, but she didn't find she minded it. It was sort of a tangible reminder that she wasn't all by herself here. She had people to take care of, and people who were helping, and people who were probably somewhere in the middle.

They saw the first body after about 20 minutes. They were getting into the city proper, and the next half-dozen followed soon after. This part of the trip was much quieter, and it had already been too quiet.

When they heard the knocking, the fact it was so quiet made them react like it was a gunshot. After a second,

Inez, the General, and two other survivors, a tall man wearing just a pair of pants and a nearly identical girl of about sixteen in a too-large sun dress, ran over to the pile of rubble where it had come from.

Between the four of them, they managed to move some of the larger pieces of debris, and Inez could now see what was inside. Kids. More than a dozen, from toddlers to teenagers. They thankfully appeared to be unharmed, but scared shitless.

"We got you," Inez said, moving more rubble to make a wider opening. "Is it just you kids?"

One of the older kids, thirteenish, if Inez wanted to guess, said, "Miss Synesthia is hurt. We can't move her."

Shit. "Is anyone else hurt bad?" This was greeted with shaking heads. "Okay. Can you move aside and let me down there?"

"You want to what?" Priyam practically shouted in her ear.

"Get down there so I can see if their teacher or guardian or whatever is still alive."

The children moved aside and Inez shinnied into the room. There was a fair amount of space down here, and it looked like the outer edge of the room had taken the worst of it. She grabbed an overturned chair and set it up under the opening so that the smaller kids could get up to freedom.

She let the older kids handle getting the younger ones to cooperate and made her way to the other side of the room.

The vidboard was in a million pieces, some large enough to make out words, but mostly they were just sharp black shards. She could see the silhouette of a woman under the shards, and she wasn't moving.

Inez pulled the scanner back out of her pocket, and was shocked to see that she was still alive. She'd been knocked unconscious and lost more than a little blood, but she didn't appear to have any internal injuries beyond a broken arm.

Inez picked up a piece of fiberwood and began brushing the shards away from the teacher. The floor was smooth, so this helped quite a bit. She got closer to the interior door as she did this, and she saw that the hallway had an emergency light on. She poked her head through the broken window, and stopped.

"General!" she called out as loud as she could, panic seeping into her voice. On the floor in front of her there was a blue and purple scaled limb, a severed arm from a species she'd never seen before.

3

The arm had three fingers and a thumb, and long claws that were almost pure black. It was cut off at what was most likely the shoulder, if they assumed a bipedal shape. Inez was poking it with a wooden dowel that she'd found, but it definitely seemed dead.

General Krishnamurthy was squatting next to the arm. She'd pulled the emergency light off the wall, so they could see the limb clearly now. It looked dangerous as fuck even not moving.

"We don't know if whatever lost this arm is still here," the General said, like she was making a decision. "If this was one of whatever was attacking earlier, we have to get this to authorities."

"Aren't you an authority?" Artur asked. He'd come in at the same time as the General, once he made sure that it was less than a hundred meters from the opening to the door. Guardian and Caiti and some of the others were assessing the conditions of the children, while the man and his daughter

(Gene and Jean, apparently) were working on getting the unconscious teacher out of the room.

"Retired."

"Ugh," Inez groaned. "No offense, you seem like a nice person all in all. I'm just not a big fan of the Free Earth authorities." Considering they'd tried to kill and capture her multiple times in the last month or so, that was an understatement.

"It's a free moon," the older woman said, with a shrug. She was mostly focused on the arm and not on the conversation, it seemed. "Is there anything we can use to wrap this up with?"

Artur ducked back into the room and came back with a blanket. "Will this work?" The three of them worked out how to use the blanket to securely tie the arm to the General's back. Inez took the light and shined it down the little bit of hallway they could see. The scanner hadn't been able to see anything alive nearby, so it was more out of curiosity.

"That's going to get you killed one day, cat," she muttered to herself.

She followed the other two back out into the waning light of day. "Fuck. Suns are going down." Then, louder, "Alright, we need to get moving. I don't want to get caught out after it's dark. I've got a weird feeling we shouldn't risk that."

The scanner beeped again, and the route was plotted out once more. "Looks like just over a kilometer to go. We can make that before twilight."

Nights were unpredictable on the moon, partly because it was a moon that wasn't tidally locked to the Neptunic gas giant it orbited, and partly because of the two stars of Procyon. The orbit was stable, which is how it was able to be terraformed at all, but for about a week every thirty-five days the moon was on the far side of the planet with neither sun providing light. Only the electrical storms of the planet gave natural illumination at that point. That was when the resort went into all-day, every-day party mode. Well, had. Inez had been a bit disappointed that her time wasn't going to coincide with night-week. She felt like she deserved a little debauchery after this past month.

Caiti took Inez's hand, looking over her shoulder at Priyam. No, at the claw sticking up above the General's head.

"Is that from the Hands?"

"I have no idea. If it is, then they've suddenly gotten very clumsy."

"It's so alien."

It's probably less so than a Grpran would be, Inez thought, but didn't say. "If it is a Hand, then we're either going to be really famous or really dead."

The younger woman stopped walking, forcing Inez to stop as well. "Oh, fuck. I'm sorry. That was flip. We're probably going to be fine. You especially, given your family."

"That's not as encouraging as you think it is," she said, her face half-hidden behind the long green hair. There were other shadows there, ones not caused by the setting suns.

Inez felt bad about whatever it was that made her look that sad. She had a feeling it was partly their fairly fucked up family. At least she had Artur who genuinely cared about her. She knew from experience that being family isn't always a guarantee of love.

She reached out and took Caiti's hand again. "Come on, daylight's burning."

Soon they were caught up to the front. Gene and Jean, the father and daughter, were talking to Guardian about some sport thing that Guardian didn't appear to have any interest in, but Jean was apparently very good at it. Artur was toward the back of the pack, making sure the kids were keeping up. She thought she heard him say something about the "buddy system", which she would need to ask him about later.

Within about forty minutes, they reached their destination. It was one of the few tall buildings, and it was clearly built to last. All of the glass fronts had shattered, but the foundations looked steady and a higher floor would be defensible.

Inez turned to the two older people next to her. "Priyam, Gene, let's go make sure the way is clear." Then, to the rest, "We won't be long, we just want to make sure that it's accessible for everyone."

The three turned toward the largest opening near them. As they got closer, Inez said, much more quietly, "The way is definitely not clear." She held the scanner up in front of them, and each body was highlighted. "Those kids have seen enough today, and so have the adults. We should move or cover everyone we can. The second floor has an auditorium in the middle, with no outside walls. I think that may be the best spot to camp out."

"Is no one alive here?" Gene asked.

"The scanner isn't picking anyone up, but I don't know if it got damaged in the explosion. It didn't pick up the classroom either."

Inside the building, emergency lights were casting strange shadows made stranger by broken walls and and furniture that was not where it should be. The three set about clearing a path to the interior stairwell, moving bodies and debris (and some conglomerations thereof, making her glad she hadn't had anything to eat in hours).

Anyone who had been in one of these areas on the outer edge would have been hit by dull shards from the safety glass, but at a high enough speed that they were practically bullets. There was nothing to be done about the mostly dried (and sticky) blood on the floor. The bodies being left out in the heat, but somewhat contained, meant that the air was heavy with the meaty smell.

Once there was a pathway and no visible dead people, they went back out to the group who were waiting somewhat impatiently. Some of the kids were complaining about being hungry. Inez's stomach was also complaining now.

"Alright, folks. We're going to go in, and up the stairs. There's an auditorium that should be pretty safe for the night. And then we'll start looking for food."

Priyam led the group in, and Inez held back long enough to take up the rear. The kids were filing in by twos, holding hands with a partner, solemnly. Two of the older kids were carrying their teacher on a board and being very careful not to accidentally tip her off. Some of the adults had offered to take over, but they refused.

As the last person went past her, she turned back toward the building and followed them up. The second level must have been nearly empty when the blast hit, as there hadn't been any bodies to move. The door to the auditorium had been knocked off its hinges, but the rest of the room seemed secure.

Inez made sure everyone was in the sloped room, and turned back toward the outside of the building. The floor was covered with the safety glass pebbles. Along one wall, she found the remains of what clearly had once been a bar, given the alcohol smell and non-safety glass in amongst the wood paneling. "Damn," she muttered. A drink would have been nice.

Looking out the now empty hole where the wall had been, she could see that there were emergency lights in most of the buildings and many piles of rubble. They would probably shine for a hundred years, giving the dusty air an eerie quality.

She could hear thunder in the distance. She knew it was just the night storms coming, but it made her heart stop nevertheless.

She consulted the scanner again, and found where the Free Earth ship would have been. There was nothing standing in that part of the city, naturally. But there was light, and with the light she could see the sphere of the drive core. She was pretty sure it hadn't been ruptured, since that would have led to a much stranger series of experiences. Singularity drives were hard enough to conceptualize when they were contained. Uncontained, the fourth- and fifth-dimension ripples would have been nearly impossible to escape.

Her own rig had a much smaller version of the drive core, and her experiences there made it a spot she avoided as much as was possible.

According to the scanner, this was an office building for the first ten floors, but above that were residences.

Residences meant that there might be food available. The children definitely needed to eat. They were scared and bored and cranky and were starting to get more vocal in their complaints.

They were also all probably orphans now. This wasn't something Inez particularly wanted to think about. These weren't the kids of the vacation-goers, they were the children of people who worked in the city.

Inez turned back to the auditorium and walked in. She went over to the teacher, who was still unconscious, and ran the scanner over her. Someone had found something to use as a splint for her broken arm, and a Free Earth flag was wrapped around it tight. Her head was concussed, and they definitely needed to get her into a medsuite as soon as they could find one that was working.

The Oliveiras were nearby with Guardian, as ever. She walked over to them and looked them up and down. Guardian was as impassive as ever. Caiti seemed to have perked up a bit, though that was probably false bravado. Artur was the one that was lost in dark thoughts, now that they weren't moving.

"Hey, I've got a job for you three. We need food. The upper floors here are residential, can you go and see if you can liberate any food?"

"Looting?" Caiti asked, somewhere between aghast and tantalized.

"Surviving. If they're alive, you can pay them back later. If they aren't, then they'll want what they had to go to good use."

They all nodded, but something occurred to Inez at that point. "Can you also keep an eye out for any communications equipment? Right now, we're cut off from everyone, and we should be trying to fix that."

"What sort of equipment?" asked Guardian.

"Frankly, any sort. It's probably going to be a patch job no matter what."

"I will keep an eye out," mei said.

"Thank you, Guardian."

The three exited the auditorium, and the two humans were clearly glad to have something to do. It may have been the first job they'd ever had.

Inez looked over the assembled survivors, and found General Krishnamurthy towards the front on the dais, making use of a table. She seemed to be inspecting the alien arm (Hand hand?). Inez walked down to join her.

"Need a hand?" she asked, though she almost regretted it. It was a little to the point.

"I'm just seeing if there's anything I can really identify," the older woman said, ignoring the joke.

"Well, now that we're out of immediate danger, and not surrounded by lots of other dead things, the scanner might be able to get more information."

"I've never seen a scanner quite like that," Priyam said, a little absently.

"Me either. I have an excellent scanner on my ship, but it's larger and not as powerful." Inez pointed it at the arm, and it began sequencing the DNA. After a few moments, it popped up a three-dimensional model of what this would have looked like.

It was reptilian, with a beak-like mouth in front of two forward facing eyes. It was bipedal, had two arms, and spines on its back. The spines were pointed down, like if a porcupine was standing on its hind legs.

"Is this making you think of anything?" the General asked in a way that said it was definitely making her think of something.

"It does seem to resemble that ship."

"I don't think these are Hands. I just don't think it's possible."

"So what do you think?"

"I think something equally impossible. Someone from outside of Orion is attacking here, and only a handful of light years from Earth."

"But why here? This is hardly a strategic spot."

"If we knew that, it wouldn't be quite the mystery, would it?"

"Hold on," Inez said, realizing the nagging feeling that she was missing something. "Hold on a minute. The timing doesn't work. This guy was in that school before the ship was blown up. Otherwise, he wouldn't have gotten caught in it."

"That's almost certain."

"But that ship was definitely not in orbit when I arrived, and my mechanotron buddy up on my ship didn't tell me anything strange was incoming, which it's supposed to. If it showed up in the hour between when I took the bug out of my ear and the attack, we'd have seen any shuttles coming down into the city."

"Perhaps they didn't arrive by shuttle."

"So, what, Spiny and his chums have cracked the impossibility of matter transport?"

"I highly doubt that."

"That means that he must have been here for longer

than a week."

"He could have been part of a scouting party."

"But if they had a scouting party, why attack where they knew the party was? They had to know the sort of damage their weapons could do."

"I don't think this is something a civilian and a retired General will figure out, Inez." Priyam tapped the scanner and the image of the alien disappeared.

Inez shambled over to the first row of seating and collapsed in between two armrests. The day was definitely catching up with her. The body suit was too tight, her muscles ached from all the walking and climbing and lifting, her head was throbbing. "I would kill for some cannabids right now."

"Perhaps the rich kids will find something while they're out gathering foodstuffs," Priyam said, dropping into the seat next to her.

"I'm only 27 Earth standard years. Why do I feel like I'm too old for this shit?"

"Oh, baby girl. I was born too old for this shit. But joining the marines was the only way off of Dharma."

"Oh, shit." The words were out of her mouth before she'd even thought them. Dharma was a colony within the Sol system, on Io. It had been touted as the next great paradise, until Free Earth separatists destroyed the atmospheric controls and sent the whole thing into a tail-spin. Right now, fifty years later, it was starting to get its legs back under it, but the once idyllic colony is still a polluted, thinly-atmosphered mess.

"Yes, quite. I left at fifteen and haven't been back."

"I was about sixteen when my owner died and his daughter freed me." This was an extremely shortened version of that story. "After a year on an Ag planet, I went to work for the Browns."

"A cargoist? That's impressive for someone your age and," she paused, then, "past. I'd expect you to be off shaking your ass somewhere."

"You need money for that." Then the penny dropped. "Oh, you mean to make money. You do not want to see me dance, let alone pay for it, trust me." She decided to let the implication, that a slave's first inclination would be to basically prostitute herself, drop. It wasn't fair to Inez, to say the least, except that the idea had floated through her brain a few times.

Besides, she knew a number of folks in that profession, and she'd pick them over a pack of marines any day of the week.

They heard something that sounded like a scuffle back at the main door, and stood up at the same time. She could see Guardian being pushed inside the auditorium, and the bright green of Caiti's hair next to her. She ran up the steps to the back (finding some reserve of energy) and the General was right behind her.

"What's going on?" she asked generally, but looking at Guardian. Caiti and Artur were both there as well, and they seemed to be unhurt.

"We caught these three looting apartments," said a young voice from under a helmet. She was a Free Earth marine, and carrying a heavy infrasonic rifle. The somewhat bulkier marine next to her was pointedly not aiming his own gun while letting everyone know he could in under a second.

"They were getting food. We have children here, and injured."

The marine who had spoken looked at Inez, then ripped off her helmet and goggles.

"You."

4

The marine was young. Probably the same age as the Oliveiras, about 22? Red hair in a braid, and a perpetual snarl on her lips. Inez remembered seeing her once before, after she'd knocked the marine unconscious while taking back the Company rig. All because of the data core.

She had returned the data core, but not before making a copy of it. Inez was sure they didn't know about the copy. Fairly sure. Mostly. Kind of.

"You're one of Hynes's marines, right?" She decided to just cop to it, rather than pretend that she didn't recognize the woman, which wouldn't have lasted for long.

"You gave me a level 3 concussion. I was out of commission for a week."

"I've had a few of those recently. I think you need a better medsuite."

"I should kill you where you stand, but the Colonel would bust me back to Private."

This was a bit of a surprise. "Feeling paternal, is he?"

The marine snorted. "Not likely. I think he wants to kill you himself."

"That tracks. Look, we're just survivors here. We're not a threat to you, and Free Earth doesn't have jurisdiction here, anyway. Did you bring the food down with them?"

The other marine, who seemed to be a bit lost in this discussion, pointed to a few pillow cases that had been filled.

"Great. Can you help them distribute it?"

He looked at the other marine, who rolled her eyes and nodded, and then took the bags of food and gave them to the very confused Oliveiras.

"I don't think we got off on the right foot," Inez said to the marine. "I'm Inez. What can I call you?"

"Leary."

"Cpl. Leary, this is Gen. Krishnamurthy, retired."

"General," she said, snapping off a genuine salute.

"Retired," the General reiterated.

Inez led them down to the front of the auditorium. She was still holding the scanner, which was not active, and decided it would be best for the marines not to know about it.

"Do you know anything about the ship that attacked?" Inez asked.

"No. We've been cut off from any other survivors. I'm not even sure how we survived. We were directly under the ship and, frankly, should have been dead instantly. Instead, Yumbo and I came to buried under a canopy of steel hull plating. We saw a few bodies. Parts of bodies. That was gross."

"You should have seen the beach," the General said. "We found something, though. Can you take a look and see if you recognize it?"

They walked up onto the dais, and Leary's jaw hit the floor. "What is it?"

"That answers that question," Inez mumbled. "We found it in a school that was mostly destroyed. It's real, not some kind of mock-up."

Leary had pulled out her handheld and began scanning. "It's a visual scan only, but I'm definitely going to want this when I report in." She was transfixed by the alien flesh.

"We--" Priyam began, but Inez cut her off with a shake of the head. Not telling the active duty Free Earthers about their illegal scanner.

"Does your handheld reach off-world?"

"It's tied to the communications array on the ship."

"Which is now in billions of pieces."

Inez saw Guardian approaching carrying one of the pillow cases. She waved mer over, and mei nodded and approached.

"Anything good in there?"

"Your human food is all so bland. Why are you afraid of using spices?"

"We need to talk food at some point. I think we're on the same page. What'cha got?"

Mei handed out some ration bars, which mei said they had found in a storage locker on the fifteenth floor. Inez ripped the wrapper off of one and had finished it in just a few seconds. Priyam hadn't even gotten hers yet, and Leary was barely paying attention.

She could feel the calories start trickling out of her stomach into her system. That also seemed to wake up her stomach, which was telling her just how empty it was.

"See if anyone needs another. I know I do. I don't think most people here have eaten since this morning. And make sure you are eating. You can't take care of anyone if you pass out from hunger."

Mei nodded again, and after handing Inez a second bar, mei went back out into the auditorium. Inez ate this second bar a bit more slowly, which was still probably too quick. Her stomach stopped grumbling quite so much, though.

"But it couldn't be the Hands," she heard Leary say. "We're too close to Earth, and this moon is unaffiliated anyway."

"That's a point," Inez said then. "It's a free moon. Why was your battle cruiser here?"

"Nobody tells me shit," she said, and appeared to be telling the truth. She was still mesmerized by the limb on the table.

"And I take it that you haven't been able to reach anyone else on the ship?"

"The handheld is kind of useless without the comms hub."

"Typical Free Earth thinking." Then, in a voice as dumb as she could make it, "'Let's tie all our comms through the ship. Our ships can't be destroyed. Oh, what's that asteroid do--'" followed by explosion sound effects.

"It wasn't an asteroid," Leary retorted. "The last one wasn't either."

"The last one?" asked the General.

"It's a long story," Inez said. "I need to get in touch with my ship. I've got a mechanotron who can give us more information. I just need to--" She slapped her forehead. "Did you see any random equipment in the shit the kids brought down?"

Leary tilted her head sideways toward Yumbo, who then retrieved another pillow case filled with various devices. Some of them were communications devices, but most were just random electronics.

"Alright, let's see what we have. T-900 personal communicator. High end, low range." Inez set that aside into a pile she mentally tagged "Keep". "Graham Communiques GC6903 air display. We can use that." Keep. "Altech Bland personal massager. Nice, but not useful." Toss. "Puff Bros 777 broadcast array. Interesting." Toss. "Generic micro-tool kit. Very useful." Keep.

"Do you know what you're doing?" Leary was understandably skeptical.

"Mostly. I spent a lot of my early teens in the machine bay, so I know my way around electronics. Oh, I'm going to need your handheld, too."

"Why?"

"Well, we won't be able to contact much of anyone if we don't have the right frequencies."

With great reluctance, Leary handed over the small communications device.

"I'm going to need some alone time. Is there a side room here?" She looked around the dais and spotted a door partially obscured by a curtain. She opened it and peeked inside. No bodies, a table, a chair, and lights. "Perfect. Give me an hour or so. Priyam, let me know if anything weird happens."

"Define weird?" the older woman asked, but it was rhetorical.

Inez gathered the Keep items in her arms, and then decided to take the toss items as well, and carried them through the door, pushing it shut with her foot once she was through. She set the items down on the table and pulled out the scanner. Truth was, she wasn't sure what she was going to do, but she had a feeling the scanner was going to be vital.

Most of what she'd done with the scanner previously was instinctual, but this was going to require figuring out how to ask what she needed to ask.

She held the scanner up at head-level, and after a moment, shrugged and asked, "Do you take oral commands?" It flashed red once. "I don't know if that's a yes or a no. Though you heard me and responded to the question, so I'm going to assume yes. Are you an AI?" Another red flash, and Inez felt a little guilty at keeping an intelligence stuffed in her pocket.

She set the scanner back down on the table. It was nearly spherical, but nearly is not equal to, so it stayed put. She set the items down in front of her. "I need to know how to make these communicate with my rig in orbit."

The small unit wobbled a little bit as it appeared to scan the items. It thought for a few seconds, and then showed a series of instructions. It was not a short series, but Inez got to work, pulling apart the casings for the different items, following the visual representations provided by the device.

After a while (more than the hour she'd estimated), she had a tangle of wires that would never fit back into any of the cases. The only things she hadn't used were Leary's handheld and the personal massager. She was still going to need the handheld for the frequencies, but not yet.

She tapped the connect switch, and after a short

handshake sequence, heard from the speaker, "Üdvözlet, százados."

"Connect me to Lui," she said, and immediately she could see the mechanotron waking up. "Hey buddy. What's the status?"

The mechanotron, which was not capable of audio, sent a text message. "The big weird ship is not in orbit. It stayed for 27 minutes and 34 seconds, and then engaged a (configuration unknown) drive to leave system."

"You and the ship are okay?"

"Ship at 97%. Lui at 99.4%."

"Only 99.4?"

"0.6% lost out of concern and inability to act."

Well, damn. Crying now was probably not the best thing. Once she started she didn't think she would be able to stop. But damn, did she want to.

"Lui, we're helping the Free Earth--I know, I know, but shit's bad." The automaton had backed away at the mention of the Free Earth. "We need to use the rig to act like the communications array from their battle cruiser. And we need to make sure they don't know about the data core. Speaking of, did you finish that build?"

"Finished, and running."

"And you're sure that it's not signaling anything?"

"Decryption unit is shielded against unwanted transmissions."

"Good. How far along is it?"

"58.45%."

"Damn. That's incredible. Thanks, Lui. Now, I'm going to bring in the rest of the team, so not a word about this to them."

Inez stood up for the first time since coming into the side room, and her body was displeased. She stuffed the scanner back into her pocket, and opened the door. Yumbo was sacked out in one of the auditorium seats. Leary was pacing, and Priyam had her head in her hands. She could see the bright green of Caiti's hair from one of the back seats, but didn't see Guardian.

"I made contact. Lui is setting up the temporary array right now. It's not going to have your usual encryption on it, but that's a sacrifice I'm willing to make. Come on," she indicated the back room, "I really can't move it."

Inez knew that the changes necessary to make the rig mimic the array wouldn't take more than a minute or two. It should be ready to try by the time all three of them were in there.

"Lui, this is Cpl. Leary, of the Free Earth, and this is Gen. Krishnamurthy of the Free Earth."

"Retired," she insisted, yet again. Like she was trying to separate herself from what the battle cruiser might have been doing there.

"Is the relay ready?"

Lui sent through a short looping video of a child giving a thumb's up.

"Right. Leary?"

The Corporal picked up her handheld and touched a button. "Cpl. Leary reaching out to any survivors. Repeat, Cpl. Leary of the FES Victory Over Oppression, seeking any news of survivors."

Inez turned to Priyam and mouthed, "'Victory Over Oppression'?"

"Battle Cruisers are named for heroic concepts.

Dreadnoughts are named for famous battles. Frigates are named for notable leaders. I served on board the FES Suffrage For All Citizens."

"Wow. Somehow sixteen years with the Admiral never taught me that one."

"Ringwald's last command was of the FES Spire of the Gods, named for the battle in that nebula."

"Learn something new every day. Any luck, corporal?"

"No responses yet, but it's possible that they've turned off their handhelds to conserve power. We can try again in an hour when it's daylight again."

"Shit, I've been up all night?"

"Night is only about four hours," the general said. "It's only been about twelve hours since the beach."

"Fuck, you're right. That still does my head in. I'm used to being on a rig where the computer tells you what time it is." Sometimes, even in English. "Sounds like a good call. We should all try to get some rest in, though you," she indicated Leary, "might want to keep your handheld active just in case someone tries to check in."

"Why are we taking orders from you?"

"You trust my face?" Learly grumbled something Inez didn't catch. "Just let me know if you hear anything."

Inez headed up to the back of the auditorium, where she could see Caiti and Artur sleeping in seats, her head on his shoulder. Guardian was sitting behind them, mer eyes open. She sat down next to mer.

"Do you need sleep?"

"My needs--"

"--are unimportant, so you've said. I've never met

your people, but with the exception of Grprans, I've never met anyone who didn't need to rest."

"Grprans don't have bones to feel weary. No, it's true, we do need rest and recuperation, just like nearly anyone. When we're gestating, we sleep almost the whole day. Our young devour us from the inside. Not literally, of course, but after birth, we are diminished. The birth of a Kastakallan is cause for neighbors to bring food for the mercilan. I've never felt much like eating after, but it's done out of good will."

"My mom told me about an old Earth tradition, funeral food. In some places, when someone dies, friends and neighbors don't know how to both grieve for themselves and support the family, so they start cooking. The grieving family finds themselves with way too much food and one less mouth to feed with it, so they invite well-wishers to take some with them. It was typically something called a casserole."

"What is that?"

"I'm not entirely sure. She never made one for the owners, and the scraps she got for us were usually too little to do much with but eat as they were."

Guardian closed mer eyes and leaned mer head back. "My name is IshanMondaHamorg'ah. That is the name I still use, even though IshanMonda and MondaIshan are dead. They are dead because of me."

Inez nodded, but said nothing. She'd sort of guessed that much. Guardian continued.

"My triad were part of the Kastakallan Rebellion. As short as that was. Our world has some natural resources that the Free Earth wanted for their war against the Shrouded Idea, what you call the Hands. They are as much a mystery to us as they are to you, I'm afraid. Our people fought back, the only way they could.

"I made the explosive that killed my mates. It should have been stable. It should have stayed dormant until it was triggered. It did not.

"They were vaporized instantly, and hundreds of people, Kastakallan, human, and others, were killed and injured. And all because I missed something. I don't know how I managed to do it, I've made dozens of bombs, but once this one went off, I turned myself in.

"Without my mates, I have no purpose. At least here, with these spoiled innocents, I have something I do. Something that will be my name, now."

"Well, shit. I just killed the man who owned me and I thought was my father, but wasn't. And now the man who is my father is here, or maybe dead, but if he's not dead, I may kill him. And that will be my choice. You made a mistake that led to those people's deaths. I've been in that place." Inez blinked a couple of times, then shook her head. "That got melodramatic. All I'm saying is, you made a mistake, and you'll probably pay for it the rest of your life. That's not fair. You should be free to make up for it."

Guardian placed an arm around Inez's shoulder and squeezed gently. "This isn't a natural thing for us, but it seems to help humans."

"That it does," Inez said, closing her eyes and resting her head on Guardian--on IshanMondaHamorg'ah's shoulder.

"You should still call me Guardian around the others. I don't want them looking up my name." Inez felt herself drifting off in the warm embrace of the tall mercilan. "I will keep you safe."

What felt like seconds later, a noise startled her awake. It had clearly been more than a few seconds, since the sun had risen.

"The fuck was that?"

"Newcomers," Caiti said, from the seat behind her. Inez looked up, and saw Caiti looking down at her. "More marines, I think."

Inez jumped up to her feet and followed the line of drab olive green at the front, darting in and out of the bedraggled-looking fighters who had somehow survived things blowing up literally over their heads. She needed to make sure that the marines didn't try to take over this civilian survival camp. No good could come of that.

The door to the side room was open, and Inez went straight in. A dark skinned man was talking impressively about something or other. What it was really didn't matter much, but the voice, that was important. That was important enough for Inez to do what she'd sworn she would never do again.

She snatched an infrasonic blaster from one of the marines and ducked in around them. She raised the blaster at the man where he could see her. She made a show of turning off the safely and keeping the gun on him.

"Hey, Dad." She pulled the trigger.

5

"What the fuck was that?" Priyam yelled, as two marines wrested the gun away from Inez and held her in place. She didn't really fight it.

"Family business," Col. Hynes said, feeling the side of his head where the infrasonic beam had removed a thin patch of tight curls.

"I knew those aliens hadn't managed to get a cockroach like you." Inez felt strangely calm, like this was just one more thing she had to deal with.

"I hadn't expected our paths to cross again, girl." He managed a straight face, but she could hear the sneer.

Inez turned to Priyam and Leary. "This fucker raped my mom and has the audacity to think they had some great, unquenchable love. Then I pop out, and he disappears. I didn't meet him until a month ago."

"I see why you didn't use a gun on me then. You're a terrible shot."

"I wasn't aiming to kill you, asshole. That would be

too easy."

The colonel nodded at his men, who released their grip on Inez. "Now that there is some authority here," he said, and Inez had the distinct feeling he meant himself, "we can determine what happened and what we need to do to enact vengeance."

"Oh fuck you." This was rich coming from the guy who killed two dozen Company employees without even hailing them first. He was a menace

"Sir," Leary volunteered, "as I was going to say when she showed up, she was the one who built this radio and used her ship as a makeshift comms hub. If it wasn't for her, we'd still be wandering around looking for each other."

"Corporal, this woman will only act in her own self-interest. She put you out of commission for days following the… events last month."

"I know, sir. I haven't forgotten. I also haven't forgotten that I could have been dead if she'd picked up a blaster. But she didn't. She's not a killer, and she's not just out for herself. She's been a leader for the refugees here."

"Your point, corporal?"

"Sir, a lot of the people here aren't Free Earth citizens, and they won't blindly follow the uniform. We'll follow you, sir, but they," she pointed out the door, "they need her."

Inez was now openly staring at Leary. This was completely unexpected. This was someone who followed her commander's orders to track down and kill a civilian who happened to stumble upon an important piece of equipment. (That she'd failed was largely a matter of luck going Inez's way for once.)

"Hynes," Priyam interjected. "We haven't met, but I know you by reputation, and I'm sure you know me." Why would he know this retired general by reputation? Inez found herself making a face at her recent companion. "This woman has only the lives of these survivors in mind. She could have left at any time, not even pulled this many survivors off the beach or out of the school, just took off. She didn't. She led us here, where we are safe."

"Thanks, general," Inez said. It was weird, sure, but she'd take it. "Look, I don't care who's in charge, but we've got kids, we've got scared adults, we've got wounded, and we've got no idea if these fuckers are coming back. Were they at all familiar to you, given your security clearance?"

"I don't know what you think--"

"Yes or no, colonel."

Hynes sighed. He looked ready to kick babies or whatever he did to relieve tension. Maybe strangling puppies. "Yes."

"Not the Hands?" Leary asked.

"No, not the Hands. They're a race from the space between galactic arms, between us and the core. We call them GL-782. Their name for themselves is unpronounceable for humans. We found them while on Hand duty."

"Why are they attacking here? And now?" Inez asked. "Did you know they were coming? Is that why you were here?"

"We were here to check in on the local Free Earth installations. It may be an independent moon, but that comes with some definite caveats."

"You weren't just stocking up on UV blockers. You don't send a battle cruiser for a diplomatic checkup."

"I can't disclose our exact mission."

"Alright. Fine. Bullshit session is over. Everybody, out of my office." Nobody moved for a minute. "All of you. Shoo. I need to think, and right now you're in my way."

"Come on," Priyam said, gathering the rest of the room's occupants. "No point in arguing with her when she's like this."

Inez shot her a look that said, "Thanks, I think?" The general smiled tightly and closed the door behind her.

"Lui, you heard all that, right?"

The comms device popped up a window. "Yes." She sat down at the desk.

"Right. How did I manage to get into this? This is not my year, I'll tell you."

"You're a people person."

"No need to insult me, bud. How far along is that decoding?"

"72.5%"

"Anything interesting so far?"

"Visual:"

The window expanded to show space, along with an incoming Free Earth frigate. It was recognizable by the general shape, and by the logo on its side. What was odd was the massive rail gun on the upper hull. That wasn't a standard armament.

The video blinked, and then there was a different ship where the frigate had been. The timestamp showed no gap. It was about the same size, but it was ugly. As much as the Free Earth ships were terrible for what they meant, they were at least logically the right shape. This was completely asymmetrical, and completely unpainted, with exposed components. The only thing that was the same was the rail gun.

Fuck, this was the same ship. It seemed to have fooled the sensors until it got close. The logs of the ship's activities (clearly, it was the dreadnought she'd found the data core in) showed it beginning to raise its defenses, but the rail gun lit up, and a tightly grouped ball of fist-sized projectiles made their way at nearly the speed of light straight into the heart of the larger ship.

The picture cut out at that point. But there was something that seemed off right at the end. "Lui, can you replay and slow it down in the last twenty seconds there?"

The picture skipped and the ship (obviously a Hands ship, just from the tech level and general what-the-fuckness of it) reappeared. The projectiles were already on their way, but Inez wasn't looking at them. She was looking at a second thing. A slowly moving torpedo. It appeared through one of the bulkheads. Not a torpedo chute, it was like the bulkhead didn't exist for this torpedo.

Even worse, Inez had seen the torpedo before. This was the same type that had been used against her at the waystation, by the Free Earth. By Hynes.

"Lui, is there anything you can do to speed up decoding it? I need to figure out what's really going on there."

"I shall do my best," the mechanotron replied.

"Thank you."

The immediate issue, everybody needed to get off this moon. It was unlikely that there were any salvageable ships at the spaceport, but that didn't mean there was nothing. She pulled the scanner out of her pocket, but it quickly became clear that within the heart of the building it wouldn't be able to pick up much.

She pulled up a map of the moon. Most of it was covered in water. The ocean was a few kilometers deep in parts, and there were two main landmasses. The one they were on now mostly had Garminburg and the resort. The other one was agricultural and sparsely populated. It was possible that the single shot from that ship had knocked out the majority of the moon's population.

None of this was going to get them back into space where she could get the fuck away from him. Maybe she should have killed him.

No, that's the wrong answer. Don't straight up murder somebody. That had been her motto since she was seventeen. It hadn't been tested much before the past few weeks.

She found a shoulder bag to hold all of the parts for the comms device. Scanner back in her pocket, Inez exited the small room. She strode past the Free Earthers, past Priyam, past the still unconscious teacher, past the Oliveiras and Guardian, and straight out into the lobby area outside the auditorium.

She looked out over the devastation, so much clearer now with both less dust in the air and with the suns shining. How the fuck did anyone survive this? Not just Inez, with a lucky dune to break the worst of the shock wave, but Leary and Yumbo. Hynes and his anonymous marines should be dead as fuck.

No, that was not going to help either. That was going to lead to a pit of despair and there was no time for that. She pulled the scanner back out and had it look for any spaceworthy ships, or at least mostly spaceworthy. Holes could probably be patched enough to escape gravity. Working engines were going to be the most important.

She spied a possible option, but she couldn't get a clear read on it. It was on the other side of the building, at least seven kilometers away, and it had thrusters. It was clearly meant for coming and going on the moon, and if it was at all intact, she needed to get there.

And then what? She had made herself responsible for these refugees. No one had put her there, she did that herself. Everyone else had been too shell-shocked to act.

No, that wasn't true. Krishnamurthy had been even-headed the whole time. Why didn't she let the old general take charge? Was she really just such an asshole that she couldn't trust anyone else with her life?

Not an asshole. She'd trusted Bolivar, for as much as that helped either of them. She trusted Sara, and that was... complicated. For about the millionth time that week she wanted to shout into the sky asking what the fuck she was doing.

Back on task. A ship, and enough daylight to get there. That's what was important right now. She felt a hand on her back and jumped, almost dropping the scanner.

"Oh, shit. Sorry." It was Caiti. "I didn't mean to startle you."

"What's up?" It came out a little more business-like than either of them really wanted.

"Oh, um, we were just wondering what's next?"

"Like, where are we headed?"

"Are we headed somewhere?"

"I think I've found a ship that can get us into orbit,

and from there we can get back on to our lives."

"Oh. Okay. Right."

"What's wrong?" Inez regretted the question almost immediately. "You don't have to say if you don't want."

"I like you. I want to kick ass like you. I don't want to go back to my life."

"What about Artur?"

"H-he's an adult. He can make up his own mind."

There was a bit of a pause and drag-out on "He's". That was the second time she'd noticed a mental correction on Caiti's part regarding her brother. "How recent was it?"

"Artur? He finally started last year, when he was 21. Old enough that Mom couldn't legally stop him. He knew for a long time, and we were virtually raised as twins, so I knew too. He insisted that we needed to keep pretending. For years. Made me call him his girl name, use feminine pronouns, just because he couldn't face Mom.

"If he'd just come out then, the gene therapies would have been much more effective. He could have been done in two years, not ten. I should have made him understand. Like ripping off a bandage and getting it over with."

"That wasn't your call," they heard from back toward the auditorium. It was Artur, with Guardian.

"It's my fault," Inez said, reaching out to the young man. "I pressed."

"No, I mean, I had my reasons for waiting. You know that, and you still blame yourself."

"I'm sorry," Caiti said, tears coming now.

"Stop it, you ding-dong." Artur wrapped his sister in his arms. "What brought this on, anyway?"

"We should be dead. Everyone around us was dead."

"We're not."

Inez backed up a bit, but Guardian placed hands on each of their shoulders, and brushed Caiti's hair out of her face.

"I think I've found a way to get us out of here," Inez said after a few minutes. All three heads snapped in her direction. "I need to get to the opposite side of the building, though. Come with me."

The four made their way to the staircase and climbed up to the third floor. This had been office space, and it was now just an open floor plan with no walls. Inez led them to the open space looking away from the epicenter of the explosion and pulled out the scanner.

She had it pull up all the information it could about the vessel. It was a transport of the sort that the resort used to bring people down from the orbiting arrival station. It had space for fifty people. It also had hull damage (fixable, she thought), and thrusters that were really old (maybe fixable, given the right tools).

Even better, it looked to be in a machine shop, which meant that the tools might just be there. Inez looked at the other three with some enthusiasm (or possibly manic glee, she wasn't sure how she was coming across to them). They were noticeably less enthusiastic.

"You're trying to get us killed again?" Caiti asked, a strange mix of wonder and incredulousness in her eyes.

"We weren't killed before, so it would be the first time on that. Sorry, wrong emphasis. I know how to fix ships like this one. Anything with a singularity drive would be too complex, but a planet hopper? I used to work on them all the time."

"You talk like a grizzled veteran," Artur said with some disbelief. "You're under 30, right?"

"27, in fact. But you know what? I spent the time from when I was 11 to when I was 16 as a slave in the mechanic shop. Then I killed my owner, who I thought was also my father, only to find out that my actual father was still alive and possibly an even bigger asshole."

The two humans stared at her, open mouthed, brows furrowed, using the exact same expression. Yes, definitely siblings.

"Sorry, didn't meant to dump that on you. I just want you to know that you can trust me on repairing this shuttle and getting you out of here safely."

"You killed…" Caiti trailed off.

"It was self defense. Mostly. Um, maybe don't go blabbing that part around. I was a slave at the time, so it would have been extremely illegal and not just sort of illegal."

Guardian spoke up then. "We all do things we aren't proud of." Mei nodded mer head sagely. This actually had what Inez believed to be the intended effect and snapped the other two out of the reverie.

"What galls me is that I have to share this with the marines. I don't trust them. At all."

"Can we do anything about that?" Artur asked.

"I am technically a Free Earth citizen, though my job keeps me reasonably distant from them most of the time. I assume the two of you are as well?" Nods came from the humans. "And you, Guardian, you're basically loaned out property of the Free Earth. No offense intended there."

"None taken," mei said.

"So trying to get everyone but the marines out of here without their knowledge would require us to do things that would probably get us thrown in prison."

"So we're taking them along," Caiti offered, after a moment.

"Looks like. Suppose we should go tell them."

"Oh, no, this one's all you," Caiti said, brushing her hair back again.

"Thanks for the support."

The four of them went back down the stairs a bit slower than they went up, but soon they were at the auditorium again. Hynes was pacing at the front of the room (did the man ever sit down?), and Leary was so at ease that she looked like she might burst a blood vessel displaying her nonchalance. The military had some weird customs, to be sure.

True to their word, the Oliveiras and Guardian stayed at the back of the auditorium as Inez strode down. This was going to be tricky. She needed to tell them about the ship but not let on that she had the scanner. Again with not wanting to get arrested.

"Hynes," she said from behind him. He snapped around to face her. "I was just communicating with my rig. Did some scans, and it looks like there's a mech shop a few kilometers away. Still intact. I think that's our best place to try and find a ship to get out of here."

"And why--"

"No, that's the thing. I'm calling the shots. Yeah, you're older, more command experience, probably better with a gun. But I'm pretty sure that you have code you need to follow. You may be a cold blooded murderer when the orders come, but legally you can't just leave these people to die if you can save them. Neither can I."

"How does that put you in charge?"

"Because I don't trust you, but you've got the guns. You don't trust me, though I've never given you a reason not to. Still, you don't, but these people seem to. We don't need to be enemies, Hynes. Not today, anyway."

The marine was clearly weighing his options here. Right now, though, he really didn't have any. Inez knew the Free Earth military code of conduct required them to render aid, and to not do so was a court-martial offense. And in the Free Earth, dereliction of duty was punishable by death.

She held out her hand. "Truce?"

Hynes looked at it, closed his eyes, and took it. They shook.

6

Now with food, water, and what clothes they could scavenge from the apartments above, about three dozen civilians and marines left the shelter of the skyscraper. The air was hotter today, and the suns loomed noticeably larger in the sky. The moon's orbit was taking it closer to the suns. It would be a few more weeks until it was back on the dark side of the planet.

They'd been going slow because even though the kids had lots of energy, many of them had very short legs and shorter attention spans. Inez was sure she'd never been that small. Or that annoying.

That wasn't fair to them, and they were doing much better than some of the adults, who were still in shock. Most of the adults were tourists, and likely they had never been more than a few hours without info feeds or holos or any of the other distractions. No frame of reference for your entire world disappearing in a flash.

Artur had been going around and talking to many of

them. He'd told Inez some of their stories. They were retirees, or on their first ever vacation, or this trip was a gift. Some had been coming here for decades. Gene and Jean were there, with Jean's mother and little brother (deceased), celebrating that she'd gotten into the university she wanted. Despite that, the two of them were probably in the best spirits. They at least had each other.

It would be incorrect to suggest that the marines were in poor spirits. Other than Leary, she hadn't seen any indication that they had emotions. Inez wondered, not for the first time, if they had the sort of invasive shit that the Earth residents had jammed in their heads. Maybe Leary's was faulty. (Maybe the concussion Inez gave her jogged some sense into her head.)

Inez was getting tired of brown. Considering how often she saw the color (she did work for the Browns, after all), she didn't think she could get quite so sick of it. But everything here was brown. The pavement was brown. The rocks were brown. The blown-out buildings were brown. The two-day-old corpses were brown. It was a lot.

Bright green came into view as Caiti stepped ahead of her and turned around.

"Don't think I'm going to let you get away from what I said. Saving our asses doesn't mean I'm going to stop bugging you."

"Which, that you like me? Or that you want a boring job like mine?"

"You don't seem like the boring job type."

"I would be so happy to get back to boring, let me tell you. For a decade, all I did was carry stuff from one place to another. The pay was middling, but usually I didn't have to deal with people unless I wanted to."

"Are you actually trying to tell me you're an introvert?"

Inez realized Caiti was perky. Unusually perky, based on the last day or so. "Did you find caffeine pills and not share them?"

"Better." She held up a bag of small, shiny, brown sweets. Inez's eyes almost bulged out of her head.

"Are those?"

"Beans. Real coffee beans. The high test ones, with cinnamon and chocolate and sugar."

"How many have you had?"

"Three?"

"Beans?"

"Three small handfuls."

"Sweet gods defend us. No wonder you're vibrating. You need to go easy on those. But give me some. I need the buzz." Caiti held the bag open for Inez to grab a few. "Also, do not tell the marines about them, or you'll never see them again."

The chocolate was dark, the cinnamon was spicy (and she was pretty sure there was some cayenne or something else), and the coffee was the most incredible thing she'd ever tasted. (She was open to the idea that her perception was a little skewed by the current events.)

"That is the shit. I could marry you right now."

Caiti giggled, planted a kiss on Inez's cheek, and bounced away toward her brother and Guardian. Inez shook her head and chuckled. *That girl is trouble.*

The older students had been trading off carrying the stretcher with their teacher on it. If she didn't get medical attention soon, she might have permanent brain damage. With medical technology where it was, that outcome would be highly unusual, but this was definitely an unusual situation. At the front right now was a girl named Kierstin, and at the back a boy whose name Inez couldn't remember. They still wouldn't let any of the adults, including the marines, carry her.

The attitude of their troupe was a bit less gloomy, with the prospect of getting off the moon seeming like it would come to pass. They weren't all as happy as Caiti, which was probably a good thing.

She popped the last three coffee beans into her mouth and crunched them. She was glad they had water, since the last thing she wanted was to get dehydrated, but she waited a bit and just let the coffee taste sit on her tongue.

They had another three hours of sunlight, and it would probably take that long to make it to the mech shop. She wished, not for the first time, that Lui was there to help get the shuttle spaceworthy. But he wasn't there, and she was, so she would just need to remember everything she'd ever learned about engines.

The scanner hadn't been able to see specifics on the thrusters while they were at the skyscraper, beyond their general age. What she knew is that it would be one of three kinds.

Inversion thrusters used dark matter filaments, the same sort used for gravity plating, to repel against gravity. Inez was unclear on the science of it, but she had some experience reconnecting the filaments. It seemed unlikely that something that old would have what was still fairly cutting edge tech, but hope springs eternal.

Hydrogen thrusters used oxygen and hydrogen to power a physical thrust from the energy of turning them into water. It was extremely safe and nearly impossible to fuck up the mechanics of it. These thrusters had been in use for centuries. Luck said these would not be the sort of engines on the shuttle.

The third option was even older than the water thrusters. Solid chemical fuel boosters were basically bombs that used a small aperture to apply thrust, and the basic concept was thousands of years old. They were also liable to do what bombs wanted to do, and blow up spectacularly.

Ninety percent of what she'd worked on for the Admiral's shop were water thrusters. Plenty of good, modern shuttles used them because they were a lot less expensive to maintain. Just as long as the reaction remained a controlled reaction, you were good. If the intermix chamber got flooded, it could turn a modern shuttlecraft into abstract art.

(Inez realized that she was cataloging things using a lot of the terms that Moses used in the mech shop. Moses was 80 if he was a day more than a decade ago, and he could pull apart an engine with his eyes closed. She hadn't kept in touch with anyone from the compound, even Sara until a week ago, but she wondered if he was still out there.)

One of the suns got very dark suddenly, and Inez turned toward it, expecting to see another ship (or the same ship on a return visit), but this appeared to be a large bird. She couldn't really get a fix on its size, with nothing to compare it to. She thought it had to be fairly large, to block that much of the smaller star, but it could just be flying closer than she would have expected. It was probably some sort of carrion bird. They would be feasting for a bit, she was sure.

"I didn't realize this moon had complex land life," Priyam said from next to her.

"Maybe they're usually on the other continent. I imagine something going after the dead would be able to scent it from a long way off."

"Perhaps. I didn't get a good look at the coloring."

"Are you a birder?"

"No, but I look things up all the time. Or I did, with the Free Earth resources I used to command."

"Research? That's a surprise. They didn't mind you spending time on that?"

"Well, if I turned up anything on the Hands or anyone else that was dangerous, they were happy to take my work."

"What do you know about them?"

"The Hands? Mostly, I know that it's impossible to have a firm opinion about them."

"I've got a firm opinion. They don't make any fucking sense."

"They are logical. I'd say to a fault, but we haven't found a fault yet."

"Militarily they make sense. They have tech, they make things go boom, nobody survives. But why? Have they ever taken resources from the colonies they destroy? Set up their own outposts? No, they wipe us out and split, which makes me think they hate us. Hate the idea of us.

"So fine, we suck, I get it. Still, it's just so fucked up. Sometimes I don't know if I believe they're real."

The general chortled at that. "I've fought their ships and was lucky to get away. They're real, alright."

Alright, it didn't seem like she had any inkling of

what was on the video Lui had showed her, because that was the only conclusion Inez was coming to.

"You know that they use the fear of the Hands to justify virtually everything they do, right?"

"I get the feeling you've seen the short end of just about every stick."

"It's not even me. I mean, I can almost understand the appeal of slavery when it's someone else being enslaved. I had to make a delivery to Earth recently, and there was some kind of security event." Inez had been that event, but keeping it vague. "The people in the city have implants that froze them in place while they conducted their search. The cost of living on our own fucking planet."

"I have actually never been to Earth."

"Eh, it's kind of a shithole. But it's instructive." A ping went off. "We must be getting close."

"Procyon A is setting, so that seems about right."

"I've been here a week and I cannot get it in my head which is A and which is B."

"A is the big bright one. B is the smaller one that seems less bright."

"I assume you already know there's a ship at the mech shop."

"I had figured. But so did they," the older general said indicating the marines who were flanking the refugees. "They're not so dumb as you would believe."

"How well do you know ships?"

"Unless it's military, I have no idea."

"This one is definitely not military. The scanner showed it as an older planet hopper, not all that different from the ferries that bring people up and down from the station.

But much older. I won't know until we get there if it can even be fixed, let alone if it will fit all of us."

That seemed to put an end to the conversation. Inez kept ruminating over everything. If the Hands ship that destroyed the dreadnought on that mostly unused shipping lane was actually a Free Earth ship, why disguise it as a Hands ship to begin with? The appearance of a Hands ship would immediately put the dreadnought on high alert and give them a half a chance to fight or escape. She knew that nobody had escaped.

This assumed that it wasn't the other way around, and it came in as a Free Earth ship, and then dropped the sensor fake. But no, the ship had launched one of those radioactive pulse torpedoes. And unless the Hands had some kind of matter phasing technology, it wouldn't have been able to pass through solid bulkhead. (Also, if they had matter phasing technology, it wouldn't be taking decades to wipe out the humans.)

A piercing cry punctuated the mostly silent street where they walked. It sounded somewhere between a raptor's screech and a lion's roar. The marines were all instantly holding their weapons, while the kids were looking like they were about to lose their shit again.

Inez realized she was standing with her arms out, hands pointed up slightly making sure everybody knew to stay calm. She herself was not calm, but she did what she could to fake it.

They saw the bird coming in from the direction of the mech shop. Fuck, of course. It was a lot larger than she had anticipated, at least twenty meters wing to wing, with a skinny body and some exoskeleton along its back sticking out over its sides. Almost like…

"Hand-holds." Hynes was standing next to her (how did he move that silently) and also appraising the giant bird. "That fits in with the idea that they genetically engineer their ships."

"So we know about them, they know about us, why come here of all places to make an attack? They're practically at Earth." After a second, she continued, "No, you don't have to answer that. It was rhetorical. Have there been battles out there between them and the Free Earth?"

"Nothing serious."

"Applying the grain of salt, you probably mean it wasn't serious for us, but they got their asses handed to them?"

"I can't say more than I have already."

"You never have said why you killed all of the Company employees at the waystation. Also, when did the Free Earth start using rad-pulses to kill their own citizens?"

Hynes actually rolled his eyes. Inez had a sense that he didn't tend to get a lot of questions. If there were some kind of governing body interested in justice, that would probably be different.

"Fine. Whatever. We don't seem to be in any immediate danger. Let's get back on the move. It shouldn't be long now."

Hynes gestured to his marines, and they started moving forward again, but kept their guns out. Guardian and Priyam were both getting everyone back up.

"I hate feeling like there's something I'm missing," she said under her breath as their forward movement gained speed.

"Missing about what?" Artur asked from behind her. He was apparently also partaking of the beans, based on the rushed air of his question.

"So, if the first time that the GL whatevers showed up on this moon, they blew the battleship to kingdom come, how was one of them caught in it to lose their arm in the aftermath?"

Artur opened his mouth to say something, then closed it, opened it again raising his finger, closed it, then scowled. "I'm sorry, you just broke my brain there. Fuck, I didn't even think of that."

"Yeah, it was escaping me, too. There's a lot here that makes no fucking sense, and the fact that I can calmly think about it without the hundreds of thousands of dead people intruding either means I'm a terrible person, or I'm more fucked up than I thought. Or both, let's not discount that possibility."

"You're not a terrible person. You're focused on getting everyone to safety, which is necessarily crowding some other things out. We only get so much space up here," he pointed at his forehead, "and yours doesn't have room for that right now."

"So how are you compartmentalizing all this?"

"Right now, caffeine. Later, lots of booze."

"Are you okay about Caiti before?"

"It's an old argument. The law where we come from gives us no rights at all until we're 20. Even though we were conceived the old-fashioned way, because mom used an exowomb we're legally considered clones. The laws are written very stupidly."

"You don't have to convince me of that."

"I suppose not. 16 is the emancipation age for those born normally. At age 20, we're finally allowed the rights of adult humans."

"That sucks," Inez said. "I guess everyone's got a fucked up story."

"Caiti is older than me by three months. She's been protecting me my whole life. But on this one thing, she wanted me to come forward sooner. If had before I had any rights, I honestly don't know what mom would have done. She's not a nice person. Now that she can't stop me, she's supposedly on board, but…" He trailed off and shrugged.

"Family. It's a blaster to the face some times."

They reached the top of a rise, and beyond it, looking almost pristine amid the broken buildings, was the mech shop. She could see broken windows and a door off its track, but the walls were solid and, more importantly, they could get in. It was squat and wide, with a second floor over about half of the shop.

"Alright, folks. We're going to head inside, see what's there. See if anybody has squatted or needs medical attention. Have some water, eat a snack, we'll be in shelter before nightfall." She walked over to the marines.

"Exalted leader, what is your plan?" Hynes was really pissy when he didn't get his way. He must have been a peach as a junior lieutenant.

"I'll take Leary. We'll go in unarmed. If anyone is in there, we don't want to be a threat. We're in the same shit salad. We'll see what the situation is, and if all's well, I'll call to you from the upper level."

"And?"

"And if it's not well, I'll call to you from the lower

level. Be ready, but don't be an asshole. I know that's hard for you."

Inez turned her back on the man before seeing his reaction. She did notice some not-well-hidden lip-biting from a number of the marines, though.

"Alright, Leary. Let's get inside."

7

"For what it's worth, I am sorry about the concussion."

Inez and Leary were going room to room together.

"I'm just glad you didn't decide to space us all. It would have been easy to do."

"You don't know me, so I'll assume that's just how you're trained to look at things. But I don't kill people voluntarily." Anymore, she added in thought.

Leary pushed a door open and poked her head into the closet behind it, and shook her head. Nobody there. "Hynes told us to be ready for anything, that you'd killed some admiral and gotten away with it."

"I protected myself from a belligerent drunk is what I did. That I also hated the man and that he'd killed my mother were just extenuating circumstances."

"You were owned at the time, so the self-defense doctrine wouldn't have applied, and if your mother was a slave, her death wouldn't have been a crime."

Inez pushed open the next door, which appeared to be a small waiting room. No one was there, either. "All true."

"That's some bullshit."

"Your lips to the gods' ears."

"You're Devataonic?"

"I believe. I'm not exactly devout. Or practicing. Or doing a lot more than cursing the gods."

"Sounds like most Devataonics I know. I'm more of a militant agnostic."

They reached the door to the repair bays, which was already open.

"I'm not familiar with that one."

"Basically, I am absolutely sure that I have no fucking idea."

Inez snorted a laugh in spite of herself. In the gigantic, mostly empty room, it echoed. The shuttle was at the opposite end of the room. "Well, there she is."

She was an ancient thing. At least a hundred years since she was built, but for that looked to be well cared for. Inez strode over to the terrestrial entrance, on the port side. It was a door that was held shut by the interior air pressure when it was in vacuum and swung inward. It was shut right now, and locked.

The shuttle was three meters from floor to top, and twenty meters long. From here, she couldn't see the engines, whether they'd been upgraded since it was built. She really hoped they had.

"Alright. Starboard side has an airlock, that's probably also going to be locked as well. Can you give me a boost up?"

"You're going on top?"

"There is a way in that is almost never locked. But I'm not that tall, and there's no ladder here." She pointed at a spot on the hull that had brackets at even points but nothing attached to them.

"Oh, this could go horribly," Leary said, but she knelt in front of Inez, who climbed up onto her shoulders. The marine carefully stood up, and Inez fell forward onto the ship. Leary got her hands under Inez's boots and pushed her up another half meter, which was just enough for Inez to grab hold of a short railing and pull herself up.

"Nothing to it," Inez said, a bit short of breath. She got up to a kneeling position and looked around the scorched and scarred metal of the upper hull. They didn't bother buffing up here since nobody ever saw it. She shinnied toward the bow. She probably would have been safe to walk it, since it was about six meters across, but she didn't want to press her luck more than she had already.

She found the manual entry box and spun the latch. The hatch (just about large enough for her to get through) swung down, and a ladder dropped from its side. "Fuck yeah," she said, and started climbing down.

The interior was dark, which gave her a bad feeling about the state of the batteries. She pulled the scanner out of her pocket and had it give the ship a good once-over. (She felt a little bad about hiding it from Leary, but she'd already admitted a capital offense in front of her, so a second was probably too far to push.) It projected information about the ship onto the impacted sections.

Inez went to each of the sections that reported a hull breach for a look. There were a half-dozen or so, none bigger than a hairline, but any of them enough to doom them. She made a note of where the batteries were and their charge level (5%, which was no good), the engine access panel (behind the tiny lavatory at the back) and the engine type (solid chemical fuel).

She heard a bang on the interior door, and quickly stuffed the scanner in her pocket. She opened the door.

"Did you not hear me knocking and calling?"

"In fact, no, I didn't. The double hulls seem pretty good."

"How is it?"

"It'll probably take half a day to get it so it doesn't kill us on takeoff, so not too bad."

"I'll take your word on that. We should probably go upstairs and signal the rest to come in."

Right, everyone else. "Did you see any stairs?"

Leary pointed to the corner of the bay, where large, glowing letters read "STAIRS".

"Exactly where I wasn't looking. Story of my life."

The two crossed the room and Inez opened the door to the stairwell. They appeared to be concrete and undamaged, like a lot of this building. Inez was starting to feel like luck was, at least a little bit, on her side.

On the second floor, more offices lined either side of the hallway, with a ramp up about halfway down. That must be going above the repair bay. Neither one made their way to it immediately, but instead took each door individually. Inez opened the first, with no one there. Leary the second, again no one. They continued this way until the fifth door, which Inez opened and stopped.

Staring back at her, eyes wide and lidless, skin covered in blue and purple scales and small feathers, was one of the aliens that blew up the city. It wasn't attacking, though. It was injured, and even if the anatomy wasn't the same, it looked like it was hurt bad. Purple blood was covering what had been a white coverall.

She heard Leary approaching, and couldn't decide whether to shut the door or show the marine. In the end, there wasn't really any choice, as she felt Leary reach for a gun that wasn't there.

"Stand down," Inez hissed at her. "It's in no condition to attack." She turned back to the alien. "Can you speak English?"

The alien being touched a small box on its uniform, which lit up.

"We can communicate," it said. Really, it said something with clicks and growls, but the box seemed to be a translator.

"My name is Inez. This is Leary. Was it your people who attacked this world?"

"No, never. My kind attacked, but not my people."

"What--?" Leary began, but Inez held out her hand.

"I understand, I think. My kind might attack you on sight, but my people wouldn't. Hers might."

"Yes, I recognize the uniform."

"What is your name?"

It made a sound that Inez was pretty sure she wouldn't be able to copy.

"Does it have a meaning?"

"She who draws water from the still stream before a storm."

Inez blinked a few times. "Well. I don't know what to do with that, but I know I won't be able to say your name how you do. I'm sorry. Are you... feminine?" She was not sure about any of this. She'd read stories about fictional and real first contact situations, but it's not like she'd ever been in one herself.

"Yes. You may call me Lacy, as the humans here did." Inez smiled, while Leary remained tense behind her. "They are dead now." Inez stopped smiling at that.

"Are you waiting for rescue?"

"My people do not know where I am. They might find me, or they may not."

Right. "Okay, let's consider the options. We can leave you here and not let the marines know about you. Or you can come out and we can try to broker some sort of peace. I hate to say it, but I'm leaning toward the first option."

"As am I," Lacy said through the translator.

"I have to ask, do you know why your kind attacked the Free Earth ship"

Inez wasn't sure, but thought Lacy might be showing, what, disdain? Disgust? Disappointment? "They were trying to get to my people."

A connection formed in Inez's thinking, then. "Your people are separate from the rest of your kind. You're outsiders? Refugees?"

"We are politically inconvenient."

Inez knew that status all too well. She sighed.

"We can't hide you. That would be as bad as them. We'll make this work." She turned around and almost walked straight into Leary. "Sorry, forgot you were there for a second. Let's get up onto the roof."

They'd been in the building for almost an hour

without signaling, and she had a feeling the marines were getting restless. The two humans stepped out into the open through a set of double doors. They found the group of refugees and marines in the fading twilight and waved at them to come inside.

"Leary, you should go meet them. I need to get working on the ship."

"Should I warn them about," she began, then nodded toward the office where Lacy was.

"No, I'll take care of that. Just start getting everyone into the repair bay."

The marine departed down the steps, and Inez went back to the office. "Lacy, are you any good at engine repair?" The reptilian's brows (are they brows if there's no hair?) knitted together, and Inez took that as a sign that she was not. "Alright. Let's get downstairs anyway and get you into the into the ship, at least. You look pretty banged up. Is it safe for you to come down?"

"It's not all my blood."

That was not an answer, Inez thought, but let it be. They headed downstairs. "You're pretty strong, maybe you can hold sheet metal in place."

Back downstairs, there weren't any people in the bay yet. "Excellent. The hatch is open. Go ahead on in, have a seat, and I'll be there momentarily."

Lacy nodded, which seemed to be an affirmative response, and strode over to the craft. She disappeared from view just as Inez heard the sound of children entering the room. She turned around to face them, and saw that Hynes, Leary, and the rest of the marines had also come in. Hynes was making a bee-line toward her.

"You took your sweet time," he snarled. "Corporal Leary says you have something to show me?"

"Before I do, please hand your sidearm to Leary. I want you unarmed for this, for everyone's safety."

Hynes's eyes narrowed and a noise came from the back of his throat, but he did as she asked.

"Excellent. Come with me." Inez turned and walked to the ship. When they got to the open hatch, she called in, "Lacy, it's Inez. I'm coming in with the commander of the marines. He's unarmed."

Inez, followed by Hynes and Leary, entered the shuttle, and let their eyes adjust to the low light. Lacy stepped forward, and Inez felt Hynes reaching for his gun that wasn't there.

"Lacy, this is Colonel Hynes of the Free Earth marines. Lacy is in a worse spot than we are, believe it or not. The people who blew up the carrier were coming for her and her people."

"Dissidents," Hynes said, halfway between a disgusted spit and hopeful thought.

"Stop thinking about how you can use her and start treating her like a person. We have to let everyone else know, but I needed you to know so you wouldn't shoot her on sight."

She pushed Hynes towards the exit and followed, with Leary pulling up the rear. Then she reached for the need-to-be-heard voice that she had been relying on these past few days.

"Folks, I want you to meet someone. She is no danger to you, so don't be afraid. Lacy?" That last was said back into the ship, and Lacy stepped into the light. There were gasps from the adults, though the kids were largely uninterested.

"We're calling her Lacy, though that's not her name. Her name in her own language is not a sound that most of us can make. She can speak to us through her translator box. And she's as much of a victim here as we are. I didn't want you all to be shocked when you saw her walking around and working on the ship. We're going to get this ship spaceworthy as quickly as possible. Anyone who can hold a hammer come on over, unless you're watching over the younger ones."

The Oliveiras came over with Guardian, who raised a long hand and said, "Of course they must stay with me, but we'll be happy to help."

"Excellent. Oh, good, Priyam's coming over too."

The marines didn't appear to be willing to put in the work, but Inez was fine with that. Gene and Jean were there (Jean insisting that she's adult enough), as were some of the other people from the beach. It felt like weeks had passed since then, but it was really about 30 hours. Short days will fuck with your sense of time.

"Alright, we're going to need sheet metal, a welding rig and a cutting rig. This garage seems pretty well stocked, so it shouldn't be a problem." Inez gestured at Gene and another middle aged man. "Can you two find a couple square meters of metal? Titanium, preferably, but beggars can't be choosers. Has anyone here worked in a metal shop?" No one volunteered for that. "Right. Okay. Priyam?"

The older woman stepped forward. "What do you need?"

"None of this is going to work if we can't cut or weld

it. What we're looking for should be labeled in standard English, but if not, the welder will be a polymer tube with an electrode at the end, connected to a fission battery. The cutter is probably going to be on one of the work benches and has a coherent energy beam emitter. Also, see if you can find heat gloves, or this is going to be very uncomfortable."

Within a few minutes, the materials and tools were in place, and Inez had the scanner out. Priyam had found several pairs of gloves, and a few sets of dark visors for sight protection (the sort of thing the Admiral's mech shop didn't concern itself with, so Inez hadn't thought of it).

"Guardian, can you work out charging the main battery? It's down pretty low and we're probably going to need most of the fuel we have to get off the moon."

Guardian bowed mer head, a dark red hand across mer chest and the other two on mer hips. Mei had Caiti and Artur at mer sides, and the three went to the obvious junction box about fifteen meters away.

The scanner was projecting inside and outside the ship where the metal needed to go, even though she hadn't told it to. Inez had no idea how it was doing that, frankly, and didn't want to spend a lot of time thinking about it. It was a risk using it out in the open, but with the marines playing "security", the risk seemed to be worth it.

(She also had access to Hynes' bank accounts. She hadn't done anything with that information, but it was there. She hadn't even asked for it, it just popped up in the scanner.)

While the others were focused on getting the hull patched up, Inez and Priyam focused on the engines.

"Solid fuel boosters," the general said, tilting her head to the side. "These are a nightmare."

"Yeah, we'll be lucky if we don't explode at some point along the line. There don't appear to be any fractures in the fuel chamber or the burn apertures, and the ducting to the individual thrusters is solid, which means the main thing is making sure the fuel mix is right."

"What did the scanner say?"

"Scanner said it was within nominal parameters, which could mean almost anything. Help me get the tank open?"

Together, they got the lid of the solid fuel tank off the base. Inside were millions of grain-sized pellets, which were generally inert until ignition. "Generally" was doing a lot of work there, and Inez didn't particularly want to chance personally blowing everyone up. She walked over to a work bench, took a glass jar, walked back and filled it with about twenty milliliters of fuel mixture, and took it back to the bench.

This bench had a fuel analyzer and Inez opened the chamber and poured the pellets into it. She turned on the machine, and a stream of white fire spit out the side for ten seconds. The screen gave a readout, which confirmed what the small scanner had told her. The fuel was perfectly fine.

She turned back to the shuttle and stopped. Everyone in the garage was staring at her. Of course everyone would notice a tiny jet of burning rocket fuel in a somewhat dark room. She raised her voice one more time and said, "It was supposed to do that. You're all safe."

After closing off the fuel tank and taking out the safety blockers (things to make sure the ship wouldn't take off from inside), Inez went back inside the ship and picked up the scanner.

"The hull is patched up, seems like things are just about ready. Artur, Caiti, Guardian, can you start getting everybody onto the shuttle? We'll want to get going as soon as it's light out. Probably start with the kids and their teacher."

"You got it," Caiti said, and the three headed over to the assembled refugees.

Inez figured they could handle that, so she went to the junction box and disconnected the heavy cable that had been charging the main battery. It was now at 73%, which wasn't great, but it would be enough to run the control systems and get them in the air.

Inez followed the cable through the open airlock and into the middle of the shuttle. It was plugged into an open panel in the floor. She detached it and closed the panel as the first refugees started to file in. The young teens placed their teacher's stretcher at the back and then got into the seats.

Priyam was sitting in the cockpit booting up the computer. "How's she look?"

"Surprisingly spaceworthy. You've done a hell of a job, Inez."

"It's something I'm actually good at." She realized she should actually take the compliment. "But, thanks."

"We--" Whatever the general was going to say was lost as the guns started shooting.

8

Lacy had dropped to a crouch outside the shuttle, and what had been an orderly movement by the refugees into it was now a mad scramble.

Inez pushed past the people coming in the two doors and saw the marines, to a person, with guns out, shooting toward the entrance. There were two of Lacy's kind standing in the doorway, weapons of some kind drawn. They had some sort of shielding that kept any of the infrasonic blasts from getting to them. Instead, they were disrupted, making loud noises a bit like a cat purring at five thousand decibels.

The sound was attenuating, though, so maybe the shields were being worn down. Inez wasn't going to wait around and find out.

She ran over to Artur, who was near a group of the older refugees. "Is this the last of them?" she yelled over the insanely loud rumbling.

"Yes, everyone else is on board."

"Get them on the ship. We'll be right behind you."

Artur didn't need telling twice. He kept them all crouched and moving to the shuttle.

Next, Inez sprinted behind the marines to Col. Hynes. "You're not doing anything with their shields. Don't you have anything else?"

"Not if we want to protect the shuttle. Grenades are going to cause too much structural damage, and probably kill us, too."

"Great. What do you have in the way of a plan?"

"We're going to back up toward the shuttle, get on it, and fly away."

"Alright. We'll do final checks and make sure everything is ready for a quick getaway."

Inez went back to the ship. The computer was booted and ready to go. Lacy was still hiding behind the shuttle where her kind couldn't see her. The airlock on this side of the craft had been sealed already.

Caiti came up from behind. "Everyone's on board except for us and the marines."

"Good. You and Guardian, Lacy, I need you to stand clear of the thrusters." She had the scanner send a message on the shuttle's computer to Priyam to have her start the engines. Seconds later, the craft began to hover just above the floor. She sent another message, "Flight check."

Seconds later, she saw the older general round the back of the shuttle. She knew how to visually inspect the ship to make sure everything was good to fly. It may not have strictly been necessary, but Inez thought it would probably help their luck a bit.

"Everything looks ready to go."

"Perfect. We just need--"

The ship shifted in its hovering like it was off-balance for a second. Then Inez realized she wasn't hearing any more gunfire. It was so quiet, she heard the grenade hit the ground on the other side of the room, and heard the thrusters picking up force.

"Motherf-- Everyone on the ground now!"

Everyone who was with her (she would take stock after the explosion) did as she said, and the grenade went off. After that was just silence.

Inez was getting tired of hitting the ground at speed. She jumped up shouting at the open bay where the ship had once been. "Mother fucking whorewelp shit gibbon son of a mother fucking bitch! I'm gonna kill you, you fucking rat dookie."

After a moment of seething, she remembered she wasn't alone. "Is everyone alright?" Priyam was shaking her head to get the cobwebs out. Guardian seemed unhurt. Lacy was, well, not hurt any more than she had been. She saw Leary on the far side of the room staring at the place where the shuttle had been. Clearly, she wasn't expecting to be left behind either. Caiti was back to having a blank expression. At least she could pay for therapy. Artur was—

Wait, where was Artur? A few beats passed before she thought to vocalize it. "Where's Artur?"

Caiti replied, in a monotone, "He was on the ship when they took off."

"Well, at least he should be safe," is what she was saying when Guardian screamed.

"Fuck. The implant. Fuck fuck fuck." She fumbled for the scanner. "Leary!" she shouted at the frozen marine. "Knife!"

The shout seemed to free her from wherever her mind had gone, and she ran over to the others while unsheathing the large knife that was often standard when off-world.

Priyam and Lacy had managed to get Guardian onto mer back, and Caiti had mer head on her lap. Mei was convulsing. The scanner was having trouble finding the location of the the implant. More than 100 meters, bad things would happen, they said. They weren't lying.

The scanner picked up traces of a paralytic and a neurotoxin, both of which were causing mer immense pain. Mer bloodstream wasn't saturated with it, though, and if they could get the implant out, it might allow mer to survive.

Leary handed the knife to Inez, and she knelt close to the mercilan. "Guardian." Mei didn't respond. "Guardian!" Still nothing. "IshanMondaHamorg'ah. Where is it?" she whispered. Guardian pointed to mer abdomen with her central hand.

She tore the fabric surrounding mer torso with the knife. She could see it now, the small scar. "I'm so sorry," she said, and plunged the knife onto that spot. Guardian screamed again. Inez dug around in mer flesh, looking for the small foreign object causing all of the pain. She finally got her fingers around it and yanked. Guardian screamed once more, and then fell quiet.

"Mei's safe. We're safe. Were there no other attackers?"

"I think they may be in the rubble," Leary said, and pointed where the entrance from the offices had been.

Inez rounded on the woman. "What the fuck happened?"

"Hynes had us back up toward the shuttle. I was on

the far right. I thought we were just pinning them down until we got to the ship, but when Hynes got on, he whipped a grenade over their shields, slammed the door shut and they left."

"I am going to kill that fucker. Oh my gods. What the actual fuck was that about?"

"He was scared out of his wits," Priyam said, from behind Inez. "He had no experience at any point with not being in control. I've known dozens like him. The absolute worst."

"So he fucked us. Shit bastard mother fucker rapist murdering shit eating sausage in a cheap fucking uniform."

"Are you finished?" Leary asked, while making sure her gun was loaded.

"Fuck!" Inez screamed, the vowel taking nearly a minute to finish. To punctuate this, she threw what she was holding at the wall.

The scanner hit the floor in at least ten pieces.

"Shit. Fuck."

"Probably better not to take the illegal scanner off the moon, I expect," Priyam said, a hand on Inez's shoulder.

"Mother fucking piece of shit mysterious tech. They couldn't build in shock absorbers?"

She looked around the room. It was just the five women and the unconscious mercilan who had been left. Inez closed her eyes, breathed in through her nose and out through her mouth. "Is my bag on one of the work stations? If I'm lucky, I can call Lui."

"Is Lui your ship?" Leary asked, looking around at the different benches.

"Lui is my friend. It's a mechanotron and should be

able to tell me something, anything, about what's out there. Let us know the rest are safe."

"It's over here," Priyam called, trotting back over to them with the cobbled-together communications equipment.

Inez took the bag from Priyam and sat down on the floor. She pulled the pieces out and reattached a few connections that had been jostled out of place. It sprang to life in front of her.

"Lui, are you there?"

A text box popped up in front of her. "I'm following the ship that left the surface within the last half hour."

"I'm not on the ship."

"Yes, your signal is coming from the surface."

"I need another exit plan. Do you see any other options near us?"

"The surface lander from the alien attackers is nearby and doesn't appear to be crewed."

Inez turned to Lacy. "Will that ship have an interior? If it's the one I'm thinking of, it was carrying the crew on the outside."

"Yes. There should be room for us, though it will be cramped."

"Have you ever flown one?"

"I am not a pilot."

"Alright. I think between us, we ought to be able to figure out the controls. They can't be that weird, right?"

"What about Guardian," asked Priyam. "I don't know if mei will be awake or mobile any time soon."

"Mei will do what mei must to get off this rock," Guardian said, startling everyone, including Caiti, in whose lap mei was resting.

"Lui, how far is it to the ship?"

"0.35 kilometers." Lui also provided a map showing where they needed to go.

"Excellent. Let's get our stuff and get out."

Within a few minutes, they had managed to collect the few things they would be taking with them, and Inez and Lacy headed the group, with Guardian and Caiti in the middle, and Leary and Priyam at the rear.

The white dwarf was rising, looking like a moon, and the Neptunic gas giant they were orbiting was on the other side of the sky, massive and looming. It was a sight that didn't help Inez's feeling of being so very small against an unfathomably large universe.

To get her mind off the subject, she turned to her walking companion. "How did you end up here, of all places?"

"My people, who I believe now are mostly dead, ran away from the Hegemony. Our worlds are between the galactic belts and we have few stellar neighbors, but that has allowed them to impose a racist minority rule. My people are the majority, but we lack the wealth that can lead to true political power, so we are shut out."

"Sounds a lot like Earth."

"So I have learned. A small group of us left our world in search of outside help for our cause. So far we haven't found it. We came here seeking asylum, which we would have been granted if the Predator hadn't found us."

"Is the Predator the ship?"

"It is the ship, and it is the commander. They are one and the same. The ship has a crew, but they are slaved to the mind of the commander the way the ship is. The ground soldiers are the only ones who can leave the ship once they are bonded."

"Fucking hell, that sounds awful."

"The crew will die if they are taken from the ship, so instead they die on the ship."

"We're not going to need to worry about that with this lander, are we?"

"I honestly don't know."

Inez suppressed a shudder. "Sometimes, I want to blow the whole thing up, you know?"

Lacy cocked her head to the side. Inez took this to mean she didn't understand.

"Society is fucked up everywhere. It doesn't even matter what society, if it's you, Free Earth, the Utopias, it's all fucked up. Feels like we need a reboot."

"To extend your analogy, a reboot is probably not enough without an entirely new software suite to control it."

They turned a corner onto what appeared to have once been a playground, but was now a graveyard of twisted plastics and metals. A large ship that looked like a bird sat in the middle.

Up close, it looked less bird-like. There were feathers, but also fine hairs. Inez could see the open doors to the interior, leading out to the personnel jump-off points.

Lacy walked up to the ship's flank and trilled. She continued forward to the head of the ship, cooing and clicking and it seemed to Inez she was trying to gain its trust. She'd seen people doing similar things when meeting a distrusting dog. Sometimes it worked. Sometimes, you needed hand surgery.

The ship settled closer to the ground. What would

have been a meter and a half scramble was now barely a quarter-meter step up. Lacy came back to the rest of them. "It is now safe to enter."

Inez got in first. She was surprised at what she saw within. While the outside was very organic and fleshy, the interior was solid, with bulkheads that looked manufactured. It wasn't as spacious as the shuttle had been, but there was plenty of room for the six of them.

The ceiling of the craft was high, but not as high as Guardian's head, so mei had to bend over as mei got into the craft.

"Lacy," Inez asked as the reptilian came in last, "if you hadn't been here and we tried to do this without talking to it, what would have happened?"

"Nothing."

"We'd have been fine?"

"No, I'm sorry. I mean, nothing would happen because it wouldn't allow you to get on."

"And if we'd forced the issue?"

"Then you would be dead."

"I'm glad we have you with us, then. Is there a cockpit?"

"Organic interfaces are toward the front," Lacy said, pointing.

"Thank you," Inez said, and headed to where she'd indicated. There was a chair, of sorts, but the only things on the control panel were two slots for hands. Inez looked at her hands, then at Lacy's. Lacy had four digits on each hand, the same as the arm that they'd found in the school.

"Does anybody happen to have some tape?"

She was met with blank stares from Priyam and

Lacy. Guardian was still reeling from earlier, and Caiti had no attention for anything but the mercilan. Leary, on the other hand, reached into the leg pocket in her uniform pants and pulled out a roll of medical tape and handed it to Inez.

"I've started carrying it with me since we last met."

"I should probably do that." She unwrapped a half meter of tape, then ripped that in half. She wrapped one around her ring finger and pinky on her left hand, and then the other on her right.

"Okay, now I have the right number of fingers. Here goes nothing."

She sat down before what she assumed were controls and slotted her hands in. She found a gel that wrapped around her and was just a few degrees cooler than her body temperature. She suppressed a reflexive gag, though she wasn't able to control her face.

"That is not pleasant. I suppose it's different if you're not hot-bloo--" She stopped talking when the ship connected with her. "Whoa. I'm in the ship." No, that wasn't right. "I am the ship. I can feel everything. Buckle up, we're taking off."

Inez didn't actually know if there were restraints for them, but once she put into mind what she wanted, the ship-beast responded. "Holy fuck." The great wings outside began to flap, and the doors shut. She verified that the cabin was air-tight.

She could feel her body in the ship, but she could also feel the body of the ship, gaining speed, running forward, gaining thrust, and finally leaving the ground. She was flying.

"Does this have a radio?" she asked, and was shown a carrier wave. She tuned it in on her rig. "Lui, do you read me?"

She was multitasking in the ship. She knew her elevation (she would be out of the atmosphere soon), she could see in all directions at once. It was dizzying, but the ship was helping her understand it.

"I read you, Inez," came a text reply.

"I never asked, is the arrival station still safe?"

"Yes, the attack ignored it completely."

"Is that ship still here?"

"I have not been able to locate it."

"I don't think we should try to dock with the station on this ship. Can you give me the rig's coordinates so we can link up?"

The mechanotron gave her the location, and she relayed it to the ship. The ship, in turn, adjusted course to make a rendezvous.

"Have I been speaking out loud?" she asked, not even sure if she was being heard by the rest of them now.

"No," she heard Priyam, but faintly. "But the ship has been relaying what you're thinking. It's almost your voice, but not quite."

"Okay. We'll be heading to my rig first, and crossing over. Lacy, you're welcome to come with us, though I don't know where you'll want to go after. I won't think about the data core with the Hands attack. From there we can head to the station and catch our rides."

She pushed her mind out into the sensors. "The shuttle is docked at the station already, so it looks like everyone has gotten out safe. Fuck you, dad."

"I should clarify," Priyam said, "we can hear every thought."

"Fuck. Alright, keeping it clean from here the fuck

out. Shit."

Back in the sensors. "We're coming up on the rig. Lui, extend the gantry from the cargo door. I think that's the only way this will work."

A short video of a crisp salute was Lui's reply.

"Alright, the gantry is up, coming in beside to link in 5. 4. 3." She could actually hear the 2 and 1 read out by the ship's speakers this time, though she was more focused on the approach. They wouldn't be able to do a full seal, but the gantry had forcefields that would take care of it. Allegedly. She hadn't used them, but things were generally working since Lui had come aboard.

"Gantry connected," came the report from Lui.

"Fuck yeah. Alright. Opening the hatch. I need to disconnect from this ship. How can I do that? Oh, just pull my hands out? I can do that."

Her hands left the slots, still covered in goo. She shook some of it off, and wiped the rest on her stolen pants and shirt.

"Alright, this way," she said, and led them across to the rig. "Something went right."

She moved out of the way to let the rest of them on. She'd never had this many people on her rig at once, and suddenly it felt crowded. It was even more crowded when Priyam buttonholed her and pulled her aside.

"So, what's this about a data core?"

9

Three women, Priyam, Leary, and Inez, were taking up most of the available space in the cab. Inez had taken a minute to get out of the dirty moon-wear and back into a comfortable jumpsuit. She really wanted a shower, but she still didn't have one.

"So, start at the beginning, right? A few weeks back, my rig was crippled by debris that it couldn't avoid. While limping along to the nearest waystation, I found the wreck of another ship, a Free Earth dreadnought. In case there was some connection, I found the emergency beacon, which was unpowered and hadn't been sent out, and tried to see if I could view the logs. I couldn't.

"What I didn't know is that when I plugged it in, a signal was sent to everybody's least favorite colonel, who figured out where I was going, got there before I did, and tried to kill me to get the data core from the beacon. I'd hidden it, so they didn't find it. When we did the exchange for it, I handed it over to him.

"(I'm leaving a lot out here because it's not really relevant. There was a lot of death and torture involved. Hynes is a fucking monster, honestly.)

"Anyway, what he didn't know was I made copy of it. I wanted to know what the fuck was so important that the marines would kill employees of the Company to get it. I recently got my hands on a good decryption machine, and Lui has been running that while I've been at the resort."

Leary gave a single guffaw, while Priyam exhaled loudly.

"Yeah. Cards on the table now."

"Does anyone else know about this?" Priyam asked.

"My Ex. I don't know if anyone else alive knows." She thought of Bolivar, sitting in the medsuite, dazed, yelling at her to run. She was being close enough to true.

"And you trust them?"

"Absolutely. But this is the important part. Computer, play the video."

"Absolument, capitaine."

The video record started playing, showing the frigate approaching, changing into the other ship, firing the rail gun and the torpedo. There was a bright light, and then the video stopped.

"Hold on," Leary said, pointing at the telemetry readings on the side of the display. "Video's out, but it's still recording."

All three watched as the radiation number spiked into the hundreds of grays, and then everything stopped.

"Did you see the torpedo, Leary?"

"I was focused on the rail gun."

"That's understandable." She wound the video back

to right before it was launched and zoomed in. The other two women drew closer to the display. The torpedo materialized through the side of the ship. "Do you recognize that ordnance?"

"Fuck me."

"I'll take that as a yes. If you haven't seen one, Priyam, it's a torpedo that doesn't explode, it just emits extremely high radiation, killing anyone within its range, and doing so quickly. The rail gun tore the ship apart, but the torpedo made sure everyone was dead. It's a Free Earth weapon."

"In other words," the retired general said, standing straight, "no matter how it may look, that's a Free Earth ship."

"You're the one with experience against the Hands. Is it made to look like one of theirs?"

"Yes."

Inez nodded. "Until I saw the torpedo, I thought it was a Hands ship that had disguised itself to look like a Free Earth ship until it was too close to ignore."

"Was there actually anyone on board the dreadnought?" Leary asked.

"There were hundreds of bodies floating along with the debris."

"Fuck. Why would we destroy our own fully-manned war ship?"

Priyam had sat on the edge of a console, and seemed to be shrinking in on herself.

"Cards on the table time?" she said. "This is..." she paused, choosing her words carefully. "It's not a complete shock. There's been talk for years about elements within the Free Earth military that were engaged in questionable activities. Given his reputation, I wouldn't be surprised if Hynes is one of them. Questionable, but fully sanctioned."

"Attacking their own people?"

"The chatter was about inflating the numbers of attacks by the Hands. That maybe as few as one in ten were genuine."

"I'm starting to think that the Hands may not even exist."

"That's impossible," Leary said stridently. "No way they could do that."

"It's been how long that the war has gone on? Over 30 years? And in all that time, no one from Earth has been able to trace them back to a homeworld? No one has seen one or even found one in wreckage? We have no DNA from them?"

The three women were silent then, not looking at each other directly.

"I don't know what to do with this. But my gods."

The console behind Inez chimed at that point.

"Right, so we're about to get to the station. I can't tell you what to do with this. But the three of us are the only ones who have all of these pieces."

Inez stood up and opened the door to her bunk room. Leary touched her arm as she went by, and she turned to the marine. "Why? You're trusting us with a lot here."

"I trust you. I'm usually right about the people I trust. Usually. I'm taking this on faith."

"But I didn't want to know this."

"Then forget it. It's up to you. I recommend hitting the station bar before meeting up with your squad."

"Oh, I am not going back there. I'm going to find a

terminal and send in my resignation. Take what I've saved and go work on an ag planet or something."

Inez grimaced. "I've done that. I wasn't cut out for it. It was the wrong kind of boredom for me. Anyway, Corpor-- Do you actually have a first name?"

Leary smiled genuinely at that point, and she looked so very young. "Moira."

"Nice to meet you. You know how to find me on the net if you need to talk."

The rig shuddered briefly. Caiti, who was sitting with Guardian on Inez's bed, looked very worried until Lui popped up a display in front of her.

"Oh, thank you. I'm still a bit jumpy."

Inez looked around the room. "Where's Lacy?"

"She was looking for the facilities."

"Well, time to disembark. How are you doing, Guardian?"

The Kastakallan slowly got to mer feet. "I will survive. I'm good at that."

"We all are at this point. Well, go on, find Artur."

Caiti ran the few steps across the room and hugged Inez very tight. "Thank you. I'm going to be contacting you all the time. You'll get sick of me."

Inez hugged back. "Never."

Caiti bounded back to Guardian to help her walk out. "Will you be around for a bit? We'll try to find you so Artur can say goodbye."

"I'm late reporting back to work, so that depends. But I'll let you know. If not, give that boy a hug from me."

She watched the two as they headed out, faster than Inez thought Guardian should be walking, but she couldn't blame them for wanting to get back to something sort of normal.

Priyam had finally made it out of the cab, and she still looked a bit ashen. Leary and the general were both still in their own heads.

"Last call, soldiers. You don't have to go home."

"We can't stay here," Priyam finished. "I know. Corporal," she turned to Leary. "Moira. I have a shuttle in valet service. If you really don't want to go back, I can take you somewhere."

"Thank you. I can't serve under him if I don't respect him."

Inez wasn't sure if she was referring to Hynes, or to Brother Lin, the dictator of the Free Earth.

"Both of you, you know how to contact me. I'm usually available."

The two military women each shook hands with Inez before departing. Leary hadn't said, but at her age, to be a corporal already, she must have been in military training since she was a child, and she wouldn't know any other life. It was good she had Priyam with her.

Inez was alone now, in front of the open airlock. Where was Lacy? She was larger than most humans, so she wasn't sure if the facilities, as Caiti had put it, would even work for her.

She turned the corner, and the door to the head was shut. She rapped on the door. "Lacy?"

There was no response.

"Lacy?"

Still nothing.

"Computer, is the door locked?"

"Нет." No. Okay.

Inez turned the knob and swung the door open. Lacy was sitting on the john, eyes mostly closed. Breathing slowly. She was asleep.

Inez crept in the small room and tapped her on the shoulder. On the third attempt, she snapped awake. Her head swung in every direction, clear confusion taking over for a moment before she focused on Inez. She touched the translator box and the light turned on.

"I am very sorry. I must be more tired than I thought."

Inez chuckled. "It's a small, dark room. I've fallen asleep in here more than a few times. Sorry for the intrusion."

"I do not mind. Are we at the station?"

"Yeah, we just arrived a few minutes ago."

"I think," she started, stopped, and then started again. "I think I should prefer to stay here until you leave the station, and then can you take me back to the lander? I believe I will be able to control it and take it back to my people."

"You have people who weren't on the moon?"

"Yes, thousands of us. We will find a way."

"Alright. You can stay here on the rig. I'm going to go in search of food and cleanliness. I'll lock the door behind me."

Inez made her way out the airlock, locked the entryway, and found a nearby directory. "There's got to be something," she muttered to herself. She didn't need a hotel, didn't need to spend the euan on that. There, a gym would work. They would have showers. And they were right next to a clothier, so maybe she could stock up on jumpsuits. Or at least underwear.

The gym was a larcenous ten euan for a daypass, but the (private) showers helped make up for it. Once clean, she availed herself of the complimentary hair-stim cream and applied it to the back of her scalp. With any luck, she'd have her full head of hair back in less than a week.

The clothier did not have jumpsuits, but they did have comfortable trousers and work boots, and a whole bunch of frilly underthings that seemed impractical, but she wanted them anyway.

She located a stand nearby that was selling the legs of some large fowl, wrapped in foil, and fried julienned potatoes. She took two of each and headed back to the rig.

Lacy had relocated to Inez's bunk room, sitting in a chair that she dwarfed without trying.

"I've got some food. I don't know if you can eat it, but it smells good."

She handed Lacy a leg and a box of potatoes and sat down on the edge of her bed. "After I eat, I'm going to have to call in to my superiors. The day of the attack was supposed to be the last day of my vacation. Hopefully they haven't canned me."

"Canned?"

"Relieved me of duty."

"Oh. Hopefully they haven't. You are not military, but you have superiors?"

"Employment hierarchies can be a bit like military ones. Do your people do jobs?"

"My people value equality above all else. Each job belongs to everyone. Some who are more adept may do a job more often, but we all do what is necessary."

"That sounds like a good system."

"Mostly. Some complain when they have a job they don't like."

"I think that's just the nature of sentient beings."

"Perhaps you are correct."

"Oh, what am I thinking? I should have grabbed a beer. Can you or do you like to drink alcohol?"

"I cannot. Our filtering organs do not do a good job of taking it out of the blood."

Inez reached under the bed, pulled a bottle from a box, and twisted the cap off. "Then I won't offer you one."

Soon, all that remained of their food was two bones and two oily boxes. She took the trash and placed it in the receptacle outside the airlock. She still had half of her beer, so she kept that and went into the cab.

She pulled up her messages (which she had avoided doing before now). There were fifteen from Gael, her boss (news had apparently gotten out about the attack, and the Company wanted to make sure she was alive, which was nice). She sent a message back saying that she was alright, and ready for her next job.

There was a message from Sara, text only, but it looked like she was just being horny and not mysterious.

Within minutes, there was a video call coming in from Gael.

"Where the hell were you?"

"Hello to you, too. I'm fine, by the way."

"Yes, I'm glad you've survived. But where the hell were you?"

"I was down there. I was on the moon when they attacked. It was only luck that I survived the blast, but from there I was just me, surviving with the few other survivors I could find, until we could find a way off. I'm on the orbiting station now."

"We had an urgent job that we had to give to another cargoist because you weren't available." She was angry, but Inez didn't think it was directed at her. "They botched it."

Inez winced. She decided to change the subject. "So, what do you know about what happened here?"

"Just what's on the news. Unknown aliens who attacked a Free Earth ship without provocation."

"That's almost true. Though, also, completely wrong. The aliens are known to the Free Earth military and hierarchy, and the provocation was that the settlements on the moon were harboring dissidents. I think Free Earth may have been trying to work something out with them, though the marines I met up with didn't seem to know anything."

"The Browns are glad that you made it out in one piece. We do have a job for you, and it's time sensitive."

"I figured you would. Send over the dossier, I'll look into it once I've settled up here."

"Time sensitive, Stanton."

"Need to pay my bills, boss."

Gael sighed. "Fine. You'll have it in your inbox by the time you are paid up." The video blinked off.

That actually went better than Inez thought it would. She didn't think the woman ever smiled. She called up another vid channel and connected to the station concierge.

After letting them charge her bank account for the berth at the station (refunds for the time lost on her vacation would probably take years), she stopped them from ending the call.

"Charge this to my account as well. Send flowers to Caiti and Artur Oliveira."

"Absolutely, ma'am. Would you like a message with them?"

"Mmmm... Sorry I missed you. I've got a job. Inez."

"Excellent. We'll take care of it for you. Safe journeys, Ms. Stanton."

As the call ended, Inez caught Lacy lurking out of the corner of her eye.

"I have to get going, so I'll drop you off at the ship."

"Thank you."

Inez remote-closed the airlock and undocked from the station. It only took about fifteen minutes to get to where they'd left the lander drifting, and from there, even less time to get Lacy set up as the pilot.

"Thank you for helping a stranger whose kind had killed so many of yours." Lacy's voice echoed in the mostly empty ship, through the pilot connection.

"People are never just one thing, Lacy. If I've had one thing to learn over the years, that's it. I think you'll find more of your kind are willing to listen than you may think."

"I hope so. May the star river carry you safely onward."

"Take care of yourself, Lacy."

Inez patted the large woman on the back, and then exited to her own ship. She shut the cargo bay door behind her and retracted the gantry.

Back in the cab, she opened the dossier to see where exactly she had to go. Her eyes went wide as she read the job description.

"Fuck me."

Acknowledgements

Three books in, and the hardest part is making sure I remember everyone I need to thank.

First, for moral support, the Speculative Writers Discord server has helped keep my spirits up in these trying times. This is the first that I've written completely during the COVID-19 pandemic, and I've had none of my preferred writing venues available to me (read: coffee shops), so it's been a great help to have other writers to lean on.

Also, huge thangs to Nate, my sensitivity reader, making sure that Artur and Caiti were being treated as well as I hoped. It was my first time writing a trans character, and he helped me identify areas for improvement.

Kat Howard, my editor, without whom I wouldn't feel safe releasing this to you, always finds things I missed and helps me make sure my "I"s are crossed and "T"s are dotted.

And of course, my life, my everything, my first beta reader and constant fan, my wife Mary Ellen. I wouldn't be here without her love and support, and I know I don't thank her enough, so I'm putting it in print, forever.

JS (Jeff) Carter Gilson
January 2021
http://www.jscartergilson.com/

Translation

Less time on the rig this go 'round, but the computer is still speaking in tongues. Here's your handy cheat sheet.

Page 50
"Üdvözlet, százados." Hungarian. "Greetings, Captain."

Page 120
"Absolument, capitaine." French. "Absolutely, captain."

Page 126
"Нет" Russian. "No."

This is a work of fiction. Names, characters, places and incidents either are products of the author's imagination or are used fictitiously. Any resemblance to actual events or locales or persons, living or dead, is entirely coincidental.

https://www.jscartergilson.com/

www.ingramcontent.com/pod-product-compliance
Lightning Source LLC
Chambersburg PA
CBHW022035170626
46808CB00003B/1218

* 9 7 8 1 9 5 5 0 4 5 0 2 5 *